SILENT VECTOR

A NICK TEMPLE FILE

JONATHAN DYER

CARTA

Silent Vector
A Nick Temple File
Copyright © 2013 by Jonathan Dyer

Designed by Coline LeConte

All Rights Reserved. No portion of this book may be used, reproduced or transmitted in any manner whatsoever without written permission except in the case of brief quotations embodied in critical articles and reviews. For information, contact Carta Studios LLC, P.O. Box 311, Sonoma, CA 95476

Carta books may be purchased for educational, business or sales promotional use. For information, contact Carta Studios LLC, P.O. Box 311, Sonoma, CA 95476

ISBN-13: 978-0-9899816-3-7
ISBN-10: 0-9899816-3-0

Library of Congress Control Number: 2014943818
Printed in the United States of America

To the Men and Women of
The Defense Language Institute
Monterey, California
1981 – 1983

CHAPTER 1

BEACH BOY
Summer, 1962

His sunburn is no surprise. Nick Temple hasn't logged a whole lot of beach time since he first signed up to serve his country on December 8, 1941. The fact of the matter is that CIA agents who are fluent in Russian and German rarely find themselves stationed in the tropics, and Nick's 20-year career path has been no exception. So when his friend and fellow agent Bill Johnson recommended a month on St. Thomas in the U.S. Virgin Islands as a way to unwind, Nick had little idea what to expect. Three weeks into his stay he is sold on the slow pace of life, the crystal-clear, warm water, and the duty-free booze. With a week to go before he heads back to D.C. and the Agency's new headquarters in McLean, Virginia, Nick wonders if he can talk the Director into making him the Station Chief of the CIA's nonexistent St. Thomas/St Croix office.

Sleepy Pete's, a local watering hole along the waterfront in Charlotte Amalie, the island's largest town, is starting to fill up with late afternoon wanderers. Its large bar–three sides of a square, each of which seats ten customers comfortably–takes up most of the joint's interior. Nick hoists a sweaty schooner of draft beer and takes a couple of gulps. Perfect! He contemplates asking for the bar menu, but he has it memorized. Instead he silently considers each of its slim offerings until he settles on another order of fish and chips.

He is about to motion to the bartender when a sound he hasn't heard for weeks catches his ear.

"That's German," he thinks to himself.

He discreetly scans the patrons to see if he can make out the source of the out-of-place yet familiar language. He sees them, two men in shirtsleeves: one tan and comfortable as if he's been living in the tropics for years; the other wan, sweating, and clearly out of his element. Old habits die hard and Nick can't help trying to listen in. They're not more than three meters away on the diagonal. The din from the bar's other patrons blocks most of the conversation, but Nick is able to pick up a word here and there.

The tan local is "Herr Professor" and at times "Herr Doktor." The sweat hog is simply "Schutz." Schutz is flying out tomorrow, stopping in San Juan on his way to Miami and then back to Germany. One of them is preparing a report of some sort. Nothing jumps out until Nick hears the Professor/Doctor say "STASI." What the hell are a couple of Herms doing in St. Thomas talking about East Germany's secret police?

As he signals to the bartender, Nick smiles at the prospect of convincing the Director that an extended stay in Charlotte Amalie by the CIA's former Berlin Station Chief is clearly in America's national security interests.

CHAPTER 2

CULTURE CLASH

The courier sweats beneath the midday Kenyan sun. The heat and his nerves are a brutal combination that is taking its toll on the courier's emotional well-being. The large umbrellas covering the tables of the small sidewalk café do nothing more than trap the equatorial heat. He vows that once he flies out of Mombasa a week from now he will never return, no matter how much the Russians want to pay him. It's more than his Teutonic blood can stand.

The trip to the modest town in the interior can take as much as eight hours by car, and there's no guarantee he will find what he's looking for once he arrives. He could have taken the train, but the flexibility of a car over the misery of roasting on a train made his decision for him. How two of his fellow countrymen have managed to survive in this god-awful climate for more than a year is beyond him. Their intermittent communication makes his trip a gamble. If their tests have borne fruit then his return to Moscow will be just short of triumphant. If he shows up on his master's doorstep empty-handed, there's no telling what might happen to him. The Soviets are not a forgiving lot.

Mombasa, Moscow, Havana – not bad for a man who came within inches of being executed by the Red Army during the Battle of Berlin, a man who survived ten years in the gulag for facilitating various crimes against humanity. Undoubtedly the Nürnberg prosecutors would have pursued the death penalty had Ulrich Hartmann been older than his eighteen years at the close of the war.

Hartmann glances at his watch. The Cultural Attaché from the Soviet Union's embassy in Nairobi is ten minutes late, another offense to his Germanic sensibilities.

The waiter approaches only to be waved away by Hartmann. At the same moment, a car skids through the closest intersection and heads straight for the café. Hartmann's only chance is to run headlong into the street to put as much distance between himself and the car as he can. As he darts from his table he glances and sees the intense focus of the Kenyan behind the wheel accelerating directly for the café. Hartmann dashes into traffic and at the last second dives over the hood of a car parked on the other side of the boulevard.

The crash and fiery blast come just as he hits the pavement. The concussion is intense. Glass flies in every direction. He feels the searing heat from the blast, but the parked car protects him from serious harm. He stays down as glass, metal, brick, and body parts crash down around him. Within seconds he hears the screams of those survivors closest to the blast. He instinctively checks his pulse and marvels at the fact that he is still alive. He feels for the large envelope full of American dollars in his jacket breast pocket. Convinced that the worst is over, he stands up, wipes his brow with his handkerchief, and calmly walks in the direction of the last journey travelled by the suicide bomber, a man bent on extracting some measure of revenge for the atrocities being committed on the people of his town. The Cultural Attaché, who was bound and gagged in the back of the careening car bomb, won't be meeting with Hartmann until they're both in Hell.

CHAPTER 3

NEW DIGS

Bill Johnson feels decidedly out of place in his modern, spacious office. As the new Deputy Director for the CIA's Eastern European Department, he has had to adjust to the perks of executive status. Years in the field followed by cramped, shared office space brimming with countless files and boxes all conditioned him to the life of just another anonymous government employee. When his friend Nick Temple turned down the promotion before going on his first extended leave in years, the Agency looked to Johnson. He has no problem being the CIA's second choice. When he told Peggy that the only danger he was likely to face for the rest of his career was his daily commute, her reaction and their late night celebration made him forget all about being second in line for the job. He figures he can do twenty years of this standing on his head, and then it's fairways, greens, and pounding a few at the 19th hole until he drops dead. Not a bad deal.

The intercom buzzes. Johnson flips a switch.

"I have Mr. Temple on the secure line, Mr. Johnson."

"Thanks, Terry. I'll take it."

He switches off the intercom, presses the flashing button at the base of his phone, and picks up the receiver.

"Nick? That you? How come you're not face down in a bar?"

"Too early in the day. Maybe later."

Johnson glances at his watch.

"Too early says who? Where are you calling from?"

"Government House. It's the only secure line on the island that I know of."

"Right you are. What can I do for you?"

"How's the new office?"

"Perfect. And you can't have it back. That goes for Terry, too."

"I don't want it or her back. You're welcome to them both, and you deserve them both. Honestly, I'm getting a little used to the pace of island life here on St. Thomas."

"How much longer you down there?"

"Officially, a week. But that's why I called."

"Take two more weeks, if that's what you're asking."

"It might take longer than that. I ran across a couple of Herms in a bar. They were chatting, nothing too serious, and then one of them slips STASI into the conversation."

"Not too unusual, right? I mean, Herms and STASI, a pretty natural conversation."

"Yeah. But it smelled like something out of the ordinary. I want to check it out, see what I can come up with."

"Done. We'll put you on expenses starting tomorrow. Give it a couple of weeks. Keep me posted."

"What's new on your end?"

"Just getting settled in. Other than that, the usual. The Sovs are keeping us all employed."

"I'll let you know if I come up with anything. Say hi to Peggy for me."

"Will do, Nick. Be careful down there."

"Piece of cake, buddy."

They both hang up, and Bill Johnson starts thinking about his Saturday morning tee time over at The Courses at Fort Meade.

CHAPTER 4

SIGNS

His family can't understand it. Their son was one of the first in town to get the vaccine six years ago when it became widely available. The memory of his uncle's long struggle with paralysis after contracting the disease at the age of twenty still wears on them all. Surely their family has paid its share.

Three days ago their son's fever returned and the paralysis began, just as it had with his uncle. By the time the fever subsided both of his legs were terrifyingly inert, worthless. Their pleas to the doctors were of no avail. How could this happen? He came in for a tetanus booster and contracted polio? Is this a cruel joke? The doctors have no answers . . . that they will share.

His mother and father leave his Leipzig hospital room in a mournful daze trying to cope with the news of their eldest son's sudden, crippling paralysis. A nurse escorts them down the hall to a waiting elevator. They step in and the elevator doors close on his mother's exhausted, muffled sobs.

The attending physician lifts the young man's chart from the hook at the foot of his bed, flips a few pages, finds the prognosis and reads it. He returns the chart to its place and leaves the room, heading for his office just off the nurses' station.

He enters, closes the door behind him, sits down at his desk, picks up his desk phone's receiver, and dials.

"Kampfried, here. . . . Yes, there's no doubt. . . . 1956 . . . . It's all in the records. . . . It's irreversible. . . . Well, it means they can stop looking. They've found it. . . . Yes, yes. The same account as before. . . . It's all in the report."

He hangs up and tells himself he had no choice. They hold all the cards and have since the war ended. Madness followed by more madness. He knows there's no escape. At least his wife will be comfortable. Her call from Frankfurt means he can stop worrying about her safety.

He pushes back from his desk, opens the top right drawer, and removes the fully-loaded Luger personally given to him by Josef Mengele. Atoning for all of his sins in a single instant, he puts the pistol's barrel in his mouth and pulls the trigger. By the time the first nurse arrives Kampfried has been dead for 30 seconds. Perhaps had he known that similar reports were being phoned in from Warsaw, Prague, and Budapest he would not have felt so singularly responsible.

CHAPTER 5

DEBATE CLUB

The idea seems too audacious for any hope of success. Its brutality is almost unimaginable. It's a near-perfect combination of two of the most savage mentalities of the twentieth century: a massive and devastating onslaught–the Soviet contribution–that relies on a stunningly evil application of technological expertise–the Nazi half of the equation. The chance that the Soviet Union's cautious leadership will approve such a bold stroke seems unlikely to Yevegny Nikolaievitch Kasparanov, the plan's progenitor and relentless driving force. He sits in a small office in the Kremlin where he and two other men, both veterans of the Great War for the Fatherland, meet for one last time before Kasparanov's appointment with the General Secretary.

The oldest of the three speaks up first.

"History will condemn us, Yevgeny Nikolaievitch."

"We will write the histories. Will we condemn ourselves? Do the Americans condemn themselves for what they did to Dresden? Tokyo? Hiroshima? Of course not."

The other war veteran, a chain smoker whose right leg is buried along with 5,000 Red Army soldiers in East Berlin, asks, with the memory of that loss still haunting his voice, "And our reliance on the fascists? Suddenly it is acceptable to be in bed with the same men who brought so much misery to our people, our home?"

Kasparanov is undeterred. His logic is simple.

"We must use whatever and whoever is at our disposal to advance the interests of socialism around the globe. And this is not just a slogan, not just some empty propaganda; it is a matter of survival. Do the Americans flinch at the notion of using German scientists in their quest to conquer space? Do we? Will we wait until American satellites are orbiting unchallenged above our heads, armed and ready to rain nuclear weapons or worse down on our people? Is it not our responsibility to silence that threat by any means at our disposal? What will our grandchildren think of us if they knew we had the ability to ensure the triumph of collectivism over capitalism and shrugged because of some ambiguous moral dilemma? I tell you, this plan represents not only an opportunity, it is our responsibility."

Kasparanov's one-legged comrade puts out his cigarette. As he pulls another one from its pack, he responds.

"Yevgeny Nikolaievitch, there is no need to lecture the two of us about our responsibilities. We have the scars and medals to attest to our sacrifices in the name of duty."

"I assure you, it was not my intention to lecture you. I love you and all the veterans of that horrible conflict as if they are my brothers and each is my father. But you know the point is unassailable. We cannot turn our backs on any opportunity to defeat capitalism, or we will lose at least another generation. Probably much more."

"What are these places? Parrot Cay? Moline? Gustavia? You know that a chain is only as strong as its weakest link, and there are many, many links in your chain, Yevgeny. Perhaps too many?"

"Your concern is valid. But we have friends throughout the world, and their dedication in the face of political persecution has been remarkable. They are ready, even eager, to act on behalf of a global movement."

"When is your meeting with the General Secretary?"

"A week from tomorrow."

A moment of silence follows. The oldest of the three stands up. His veteran comrade follows, propping himself on his crutches.

"You will tell our friend Nikita Sergeyevich that you have our complete support. The rest is up to him."

The sight of these two men who gave so much for their country is almost enough to bring Kasparanov to tears. Instead, he hugs each of them in turn before they leave his office. They depart slowly, burdened as much by a past of unspeakable horror as by the specter of what they are about to unleash.

CHAPTER 6

THE LAB BOYS

St. Thomas in the U.S. Virgin Islands is an unusual spot for an experimental medical science lab. And that's why it's perfect. The fact that his work has gone on right under the noses of the sanctimonious Americans gives Professor Hartmut Schnelling particular delight. Add to that the stunning success of his work and Schnelling has every reason to believe that he will be handsomely rewarded by his Soviet overlords.

Many other men would be content with a modestly compensated, quiet life in the American paradise, tinkering in a lab on more or less their own timetable. Not Schnelling. Having taken his Ph.D. in biochemistry on the eve of the invasion of Poland, he saw a promising career in research cut short by the needs of the Wehrmacht. He became little more than a lab chemist during the first two years of the war working at various hideous "camps" on an as-needed basis. As the war progressed, his training was deemed sufficient to make him a field medical officer. He was shipped to the Eastern front in time to be a first-hand witness to the long retreat and collapse of Germany's once mighty war machine.

His bitterness could easily have been directed at his own country, but such is not the case for Hartmut Schnelling. Any contribution he can make to the downfall of the world's current, dominant superpower, a status he and millions of other Germans once sought for their own country, will bring him great satisfaction. He is, however, no blind ideologue. He is more accurately a survivor. And the presence on the island of a lone American for more than three weeks straight has caught his attention.

There's likely nothing to it, he tries to convince himself. He considered letting Moscow know, but he dismissed the idea as a sign of weakness. After all, a single American should be easy enough for a veteran of the Stalingrad campaign to dispose of, if it comes to that.

He decides to be mindful without getting overwrought, aware without letting his suspicions get away from him. Perhaps some discreet inquiries of the few contacts he has established on the island will be all he needs. The timetable is clear. The target is October. Nothing, certainly not some sunburnt American, will keep him from his destiny!

CHAPTER 7

ROADBLOCK

"You can see for yourself it's a diplomatic passport. Now let me pass."

While the Captain of the Guard is less than impressed, he remains courteous.

"Please remain in your car. I'll return in a moment."

Hartmann is about to demand the return of his passport when the captain motions to one of his men. The soldier immediately turns his shoulder-slung L52 Sten submachine gun on Hartmann who decides to save his protestations.

The captain calmly walks to the small building on the south side of the checkpoint that houses his office, a small communications room, and billets for half a dozen soldiers. The station was constructed by the British during the worst days of the Mau Mau rebellion to control the flow of supplies and men from the coast to the interior. The rebellion is over and independence is a pending certainty, yet the station, one of the last vestiges of colonialism, remains. It sits in the semi-arid Taru Desert of Kenya, across the only road to Voi from Mombasa, a trip of approximately 150 kilometers.

Hartmann wipes the sweat from his brow. The two acacia trees on either side of the station's building provide the only shade for a considerable distance. He should just reach the small village east of Voi before dusk. The longer the captain takes with his passport, the slimmer are Hartmann's chances of arriving before dark. After what seems like an hour, the captain returns.

"You are to come with me."

"What is the meaning of this?"

"What is your destination?"

"Nairobi," Hartmann lies.

"And what of your countrymen in Voi?"

"What are you talking about? I demand the return of my passport, immediately!"

"Answer my question. What do you know of the German doctors in Voi?"

Hartmann's bluster is beginning to give way to fear. The officer's questions betray an ominous fate for his countrymen that he works hard not to imagine.

"I told you. I am going to Nairobi. I know nothing of Germans in Voi. Now, are you going to return my passport? If not, I will be forced to return to Mombasa and report this matter to the proper authorities."

The captain holds out Hartmann's passport. Hartmann reaches for it. As he does the captain pulls his hand back, and steps towards Hartmann, bringing himself less than six inches away from the profusely sweating foreigner. The captain's eyes narrow to slits. He addresses Hartmann in a menacing whisper that barely masks a century of rage.

"Mombasa is your only chance."

CHAPTER 8

THE DOCTOR IS OUT

A small crowd gathers by the roadside waiting for the local constabulary to respond. The slayings are the first in the area since the state of emergency was lifted more than 18 months ago, in December of 1960.

As the crowd builds, those in back have to strain to get a glimpse. What they see is a brutal reminder of the country's recent and terrifying past: two disemboweled white bodies, faces mutilated to hinder identification. Next to the bodies, left behind as calling cards, are the assassins' grisly instruments: four pangas, the soft iron machetes favored by the Mau Mau.

A man in his late 30s pushes a wheelchair along the road. In the wheelchair is his beautiful seventeen-year-old daughter whose withered legs dangle uselessly beneath her pleated skirt. The crowd goes silent and parts as the two, father and daughter, approach the roadside ditch. He stops the chair as they peer down at the bodies. Tears run down the young woman's face. The father steps to the edge of the ditch and spits on the bodies. He returns to grab the handles of the wheelchair, backs away from the ditch, and returns to the road, slowly making his way home.

"The doctors," a man offers.

"They were butchers, not doctors," is a woman's retort.

The siren of an approaching patrol car from Voi fills the air. The crowd stands aside as the siren goes silent and the car comes to a stop just short of the ditch. A tall, angular policeman gets out from behind the wheel, calmly dons his hat, and closes the patrol car door. He walks over to the ditch, squats at the edge, and stares for no more than ten seconds. He stands and addresses the small crowd.

"Who found them?"

A boy no more than ten years old steps forward.

"I did."

The officer goes to the boy, puts his arm around his shoulder and leads him away from the crowd.

"Did you or anyone touch anything after you found them?"

"No, sir. Not a thing. They were just like that."

"Okay, then. Off you go."

The boy hustles back to the crowd. The officer walks to his patrol car, reaches inside the open passenger window, and pulls a push-to-talk mic out of its cradle. He pauses for a second before calling it in. The crowd listens in as the officer reports to the dispatcher.

"No. No need for an ambulance. I'm quite certain the coroner will do. Out."

He places the mic back in its cradle and leans against his patrol car to wait. The crowd slowly disperses. Some smile, some shake hands, and a few wave to their neighbors, all of which tells the officer what he already knew. The bodies in the ditch are no harbinger. Instead, they mark the end of a nightmare that none, even the most hardened among them, would have imagined.

CHAPTER 9

GREEN LIGHT

"And if your plan had been disapproved? How would you explain these enormous expenditures to the Politburo?" the General Secretary thunders.

"I had confidence in the wisdom of the plan."

"You are lucky to have such distinguished friends, or the wisdom of your plan, as you call it, would mean nothing, especially if the science simply didn't exist."

"Of course. It was a chance I took, but I felt it worth taking."

The General Secretary squints and rubs his temples. His very public confrontational persona is at times a veneer. At this moment, he knows that what he is about to embark upon could change the course of history, or lead to his execution, or both. He focuses on the former of the two possibilities knowing full well that the latter is a mundane fact of political life in the Soviet Union.

"We will need to divert the attention of the Americans. And running guns to some amateur anticolonial revolt won't come close to doing the trick."

Kasparanov is surprised by the General Secretary's cynical frankness. Surprised and pleased. It means he is trusted. It means the plan is approved!

The General Secretary walks over to a map of the world that adorns the entire west wall of his office. He scans the map, rubbing his plump chin as he ponders what he considers to be the missing piece of

Kasparanov's daring gamble. And then it hits him. Cuba! It's perfect. The island has been a dilemma for the Americans for nearly their entire history. Any move by the Soviet Union will instantly get the full attention of the young president and his ridiculously suspicious government. He decides at that moment to put Kasparanov, who he must admit continues to display a genius for strategic planning, on the problem.

"Cuba, Yevgeny Nikolaievitch. Cuba. I'll leave it to you, but the diversion is Cuba. The Americans are sick over Castro and their foolish Bay of Pigs adventure. Cuba is a thorn in their side, and I want you to figure out how to twist that thorn, how to cause them so much pain that they can see nothing else. Then, and only then, can your plan succeed."

The General Secretary continues to stare at the map. Kasparanov, knowing the meeting is over, discreetly leaves the room, his mind racing with possibilities for the Soviet Union's ally only 90 miles from American soil.

CHAPTER 10

ONCE MORE BEFORE YOU LEAVE

He knows it's not the sort of career that one gets to slowly wind down as he anticipates retirement. But he also knows he's having an increasingly difficult time maintaining the pace expected of the Director of the free world's largest intelligence agency. After more than seven years on the job, years that are a capstone to a lifetime spent in service to his country, he let the young president know that he is ready to step down. He will stay on through the end of the year, but it is his intention to be a private, anonymous civilian, ready to play golf at least five times a week by January 1, 1963.

After allowing himself a brief vision of life after the CIA, he returns his focus to the one-page report, really not much more than a page of notes, on his desk in front of him.

He picks up his telephone and dials Bill Johnson's extension.

"How can I help you, sir?"

"Bill, I'm looking at your notes on Kenya. How'd this land on your desk?"

"A nice bit of analysis by Hugh Ridgely, our man in Cairo. Everyone had the Mombasa bombing, but he saw an embassy cable on the Voi murders and decided to dig."

"Is he sure about the attaché?"

"He spent a little money in Mombasa and got what he needed. The attaché had an appointment with some guy named Hartmann. Not exactly a Russian surname."

"I saw that, but what about the murders?"

"German nationals. Put that together with a Soviet Cultural Attaché blown to bits in a car bomb moments before he was supposed to meet with another German national and that's how it ended up on my desk."

"East or West German?"

"Looks like the East, at least the guy who was supposed to meet the attaché."

"What the hell were they doing in Voi?"

"That's just one more thing we don't know. Ridgely wants to go back to Kenya, see what he can stir up. I thought I'd run it by you first. I don't think the Brits or the Kenyans want CIA sniffing around Kenya's interior right now, so maybe Ridgely's the wrong person to send."

"State must have some contacts in Nairobi through the Brits. A local is best. I'll see if the UK can help us out. Murdered Germans in Kenya. Got to be more there than meets the eye."

"I'll see what I can do. Anything else I can do for you, sir?"

"That'll do for now. Thanks, Bill."

The Director hangs up. As he does he privately laments the Agency's lack of resources in Africa. He's made the pitch on more than one occasion, but in spite of the region's clear vulnerability to Soviet influence his pitch has consistently fallen on deaf ears. Money for Asia, more for Europe, some for the Middle East, and precious little for the entire continent of Africa. It's a familiar story. The hell of it is that he hates going hat in hand to State and the Brits. But if the Germans and Russians are up to something, even if their focus is Kenya, the Director has to do what he can to ferret it out.

He presses a button on his intercom.

"Cheryl?"

"Yes, sir?"

"I need to speak with the Secretary of State."

CHAPTER 11

SURF'S UP

Hull Bay, on the Atlantic side of St. Thomas, is one of the few spots on the island where surfing is possible. Nick Temple put surfing on his list of things to do before he drops dead after hearing about some wild man named Greg Noll surfing enormous waves on Oahu's North Shore back in '57. There isn't much surf in Berlin, which is like saying there isn't much snow in Hell, so the opportunities to catch a few waves have been few and far between for the past five years.

This morning he rented a longboard, put it into the Kaiser Jeep CJ-5 he's been driving around the island for a month, and drove over the ridge of St. Thomas to Hull Bay. Now, six hours and precious few moments of standing upright on the board for more than two seconds at a time later, Nick is ready to call it a day. His choices aren't good. He can either paddle the half kilometer back to where his Jeep is parked, or he can take the next small wave (it's not exactly Waimea, which strikes Nick as a good thing in retrospect) into shore, put the board under his arm and walk. He chooses option number one.

As he approaches the point where his Jeep is parked, his shoulders exhausted, his salt-and-pepper hair and eyelashes caked with sea salt, and his back and face freshly burnt, he sees an islander, a young man perhaps in his early 20s, climb into his Jeep. The fact that the Jeep has no top makes the islander's move effortless. Nick then sees the man bend over to look beneath the dash.

"The son of a bitch is going to hot wire it," Nick thinks to himself.

"Hey! Get the fuck away from my car!" he yells.

The islander looks up for a second before resuming his work. Nick paddles furiously, but he's more than 100 meters away and knows he has no chance if the man knows what he's doing. And he does. Nick hears the sound of the Jeep's engine turning over. The islander sits upright, shifts into reverse and. . . . The explosion is ferocious! It throws the shredded islander ten meters into the air. His lifeless body lands with a thud at the high tide mark as what is left of the Jeep is consumed by a ball of fire.

Nick sits up on his surfboard, his lower legs dangling in the warm Atlantic water.

"Tough day to be a thief," he thinks to himself.

After mulling over his next move, he lowers himself back onto the board to paddle the rest of the way into shore with little doubt that his presence on St. Thomas is at least unwelcome and at worst a mortal threat.

CHAPTER 12

CIRCLE THE WAGONS

"Serves the poor bastard right!"

Bill Johnson nods in agreement with the Director's assessment. Nick responds on the speaker phone.

"Yeah, I think he got a little more than he bargained for."

"Any identification yet?"

"A local guy. Nothing that raises any flags. A couple of months in jail here and there. A petty theft beef and a stint for possession."

"I think you should pack your bags and head back to D.C., Nick, at least until we can get a better handle on the situation."

"I'm already packed, sir. I've got a seat on the evening hop to San Juan. I'll spend the night in Condado and head out for Miami in the morning."

"Don't unpack when you get here."

"Why's that, Bill?"

"We're picking up bits and pieces of some kind of Soviet and German activity in Kenya. Your guy down there is a professor, right?"

"That's what his contact called him."

"Two German doctors were butchered outside of Voi."

"Never heard of it."

"It's about 150 clicks west of Mombasa."

"You think the Sovs did it?"

The Director chimes in.

"Negative. But the Soviet Cultural Attaché from their consulate in Mombasa was blown to bits right before he was supposed to meet with a third German. I won't go into the details right now, but the man responsible for the attaché's death was from Voi. My gut tells me your man on St. Thomas is connected."

"Seems like a longshot."

"No question. But I'd bet your paycheck I'm right."

"I'm all for it if it means coming back down here, as long as the Company's willing to spring for a new Jeep."

"Not a problem, but two's the limit."

"I'll call when I get to Miami."

"Call Bill. He can set up our meeting. See you soon, Nick."

The Director picks up the receiver and sets it back down ending the call. Bill Johnson gets up to leave.

"Anything from State?"

"They sent over a file of a Kenyan the UK Governor's office said is top notch. Should be able to help us out. Cheryl has the file. Pick it up, look it over, and think about what we want her to do."

"Her?"

"That's right. I've read the file, and I agree with State. She's got what it takes."

"I'll get on it. Anything else, sir?"

"That's all I've got. We'll talk when Nick gets back."

"Will do."

Bill Johnson walks out of the Director's office. He stops at the Director's secretary's desk.

"Got a file for me, Cheryl?"

Cheryl grabs the file in her in-box marked "CONFIDENTIAL" and hands it to Johnson. He opens it up. Stapled to the inside cover is a photograph of Dalila Atieno, a 30-year-old Kenyan who works for the Provincial Commissioner in Nairobi. The routine bureaucratic nature of the small black and white photograph absolutely fails to tone down her stunning beauty.

CHAPTER 13

BIGGER BANG FOR YOUR RUBLE

Yevgeny Karaspanov sits at the kitchen table of his cramped Moscow apartment staring out of the room's small open window. Although he is a rising star in the Communist Party, he knows that his living accommodations are almost claustrophobic by western standards. Kasparanov also knows that as he continues to rise through the ranks of the Party elite he will be rewarded with more and more of the creature comforts true socialists are supposed to eschew. It is a fact of life in the Soviet Union that the more power one has within the ruling apparatus of this purportedly collectivist nation, the more personal perquisites one enjoys. It is also a fact of life that at any moment the modest degree of comfort that Kasparanov has built for himself and his young family can be snatched away by the sort of fierce internal politics that has characterized his country since at least 1917.

His wife, Zenaida, dries the last of their dinner dishes and joins him at the table. Tatyana, their three-year-old daughter, has been asleep for an hour.

"Vodka?" she asks him.

"Of course," is his almost autonomic response.

Zenaida dries her hands on her apron. With one hand she takes two shot glasses from the white, metal cabinet above the kitchen sink; with the other hand she pulls a nearly empty bottle of the national beverage from the same cabinet. She closes the door, places the two shot glasses on the table, and pours.

"Your daughter does not like it when her father is so glum, so stern. Neither does your wife."

"Forgive me. I should pay more attention to the two of you. I have too much on my mind lately."

"Like what?"

"The Americans."

Zenaida laughs and lights a cigarette which she hands to her husband.

"Isn't your job to make the Americans worry about us?"

"More so than ever."

"Then what worries them the most?"

"The same thing that worries us. Nuclear war."

Zenaida laughs again.

"You politicians. You worry about something that will never happen."

"Your confidence, I'm afraid, is not shared."

"By who? Ask a Muscovite, and not some Party apparatchik. He'll tell you. Both sides are so afraid of the possibilities that neither side will ever use these weapons. You can bet the average American knows in his heart what I already know. These weapons are useless except for blustering politicians to frighten each other with."

Kasparanov nods, his eyes growing wider as he does. He takes the shot glass, drains it and places it on the table. He pours another shot. Zenaida picks up her shot glass and sips the vodka, savoring it rather than gulping it.

"But if we can convince them we're not afraid of starting such a war?" Yevgeny asks.

"Well, then you'd certainly get their attention. And not just the government. The people. You'd get their attention too. But, at least for the sake of your daughter, perhaps we should not do such a thing."

"Yes. We would certainly get their attention. Zenaida, you're a genius. And to think I married you for your beauty."

"You married me because I was pregnant."

"A circumstance caused primarily by your beauty!"

They both laugh lightly. She reaches for his free hand and takes it in hers. They lean towards each other until their foreheads are touching. The attraction has always been deeply mutual, and here in the half-light of a summer evening, it is as strong as ever.

CHAPTER 14

THE HOME TEAM

Dalila Atieno opens the morning's first visa application. Her work at the Provincial Commissioner's office in the heart of Nairobi, a building referred to by local Brits as "Hatches, Matches, and Dispatches" due to the births, marriages, and deaths recorded within its thick colonial walls, is routine. The skills she acquired as a top undergraduate studying economics and politics at the University of London are rarely officially used. She is, however, consulted on a wide range of matters that would fit under the general heading of "Kenyan Affairs" by her British employers. She has a reputation for keen analysis coupled with a deep cultural understanding that makes her invaluable to the office of the Governor during this period of transition from colonial to self-rule. Her ambition, one she openly admits to harboring, is to continue in the political tradition of her forbears once Kenya achieves full independence. In the meantime, she learns as much as she can about national administration while working for the appreciative Brits.

She flips open a file just as Cecil Rodgers, her supervisor, enters her office.

"Dalila, might I have a word with you?"

"Of course, Mr. Rodgers."

He enters and sits in the small room's one unoccupied chair.

"What can I do for you this morning?"

Rodgers, a lifer with the British Colonial Office, can't help admiring the young woman across the desk from him. He particularly likes the fact that her quick analytical mind is matched by her strength of character. Without being overbearing, she has never made any secret of her desire to someday serve an independent Kenya. Her deep interest in Kenyan politics has made her invaluable to the Governor's office. The fact that she is strikingly beautiful has been both a hindrance and a help to her. Her beauty is what most men–and politics remains dominated by men in 1962–see when they first encounter her. Her lucid, active mind is what they learn to admire when they get to know her. Rodgers travelled that same path. And now, when he needs to understand Kenya in a way that its colonial masters never could, he turns to Dalila Atieno. But today's visit is different. It seems that her orbit of admirers is about to extend well beyond Nairobi's Provincial Commissioner's Office.

"We've had a request from the Americans. They're in need of some assistance on a matter that must be handled with a good deal of discretion."

"It sounds intriguing."

"It might be messy. It's about those two Germans who were found murdered in Voi."

"What do the Americans want from me?"

"Someone with brains, candor, and expert knowledge of the cultural and political landscape. Yours was the only name we considered giving them."

"I'm flattered, of course. And I would relish the chance to work with them."

"That's settled then. They've already reviewed your file. I sent a copy on to them when the matter first came up. I hope you don't mind."

"Not at all."

"I'll arrange the meeting. It will involve a trip to Cairo. There appears to be some urgency about the matter, so be prepared to leave at a moment's notice."

"So long as my employer approves."

"He does, so long as we don't lose you to the Americans."

Dalila laughs.

"You're going to lose me to the Kenyans in short order. Don't forget."

"Right you are, and it's a damned shame, too. Well, I'll be off and let you get back to work. Thanks so much for your time."

"Of course, Mr. Rodgers."

Rodgers stands and executes a slight bow, really more of a nod, before turning and leaving the office.

Dalila ponders what life would be like working for the Americans for just a moment. She quickly dismisses the idea and returns to the routine bureaucratic matters awaiting her attention.

CHAPTER 15

PLAN B?

Hartmut Schnelling has never had any patience with those elements of society he considers undesirable. Today, thieves will top his long personal list of the least desirable.

He sits in the kitchen of his modest bungalow four blocks from the West Indian Company dock west of Charlotte Amalie, smoking a cigarette and sipping a cup of hot black coffee. As he does six mornings a week, he peruses the modest local newspaper, *The Virgin Islands Daily News*. The exercise helps him feed his superiority complex. Today, its banner headline screams: "CAR THIEF'S PLAN UP IN FLAMES!" Schnelling chuckles slightly as he contemplates the fate of another hapless islander who refuses to make an honest living. If asked, Schnelling would likely declare that being paid handsomely to formulate deadly poisons for the benefit of an occupying power most certainly qualifies as an honest living.

As he leisurely scans what he thinks is going to be a fairly routine story about the fate of a thoroughly deserving car thief, he gradually comes to realize that the object of the thief's attempt was the American's rented Jeep, and that the five-thousand American dollars he paid to have the American nuisance eliminated has gone completely to waste! Idiot! He slams the kitchen table rattling his coffee cup in its saucer.

He collects himself and reads the article again, this time scrutinizing it for any clue that the explosion might be tied to him.

The dead thief was a local troublemaker by the name of Jimmy Bouldin. But there is nothing about the identity of the renter of the Jeep other than his nationality. That tells him his concerns about the American were well-founded; clearly he is a man of connections whose presence on St. Thomas encompasses more than a simple vacation. The paper would not hesitate to print the name of a generic stateside tourist whose rented car was blown to bits during an abortive attempt to steal it. If that were the case, Schnelling would expect to see a few choice quotes from the intended victim inserted into the story.

Schnelling folds the newspaper neatly, takes one last sip from his cup of coffee, and gets up from the table. He goes to a wall safe clumsily hidden in his bedroom behind a hideous oil painting of a safari gathered around a freshly killed elephant. He opens the safe and pulls out a small, black, leather-bound code book. He takes the book to a desk in one corner of the bedroom, sits at the desk, opens the book, and begins to compose a message asking for assistance in dealing with the annoying presence of the lucky American.

His concentration is interrupted when his phone rings. He returns to the kitchen to answer it.

"Schnelling here."

"Have you seen the paper?"

"I told you not to call me here."

"I want to deliver satisfaction."

"Don't be a fool. You have your money, now leave me alone. You make it too easy for us to be connected."

"I'll give you a discount."

In spite of his fears, Schnelling is intrigued.

"Why?"

"The job's not finished, through no fault of mine, mind you."

"I'll consider it, but you mustn't call me. I'll get in touch with you if I need you."

"Fair enough."

Schnelling hangs up. He pauses for a moment before heading back to his desk to amend his message to Moscow.

CHAPTER 16

MEETING OF THE MINDS

Nick Temple, tan and rested from an extended Caribbean vacation, walks through the spacious and modern foyer of the CIA's new headquarters in McLean, Virginia. Although this is not Nick's first visit to the vast complex, it is his first appearance since the Agency's move to what is already being called "Langley" became complete in the spring of this year. To avoid the embarrassment of having to ask for directions, he convinced Bill Johnson to provide a description of the path to his office during his check-in call from Miami.

As he heads for a set of elevators, Nick can't help comparing the gleaming new structure to the collection of cramped, often hastily constructed "offices" he has had the pleasure to call home since his earliest days with the OSS. The utilitarian, almost Spartan nature of his government-issue accommodations for the last 20-plus years rarely gave any hint of the resources or intentions of his employer. This spacious new building leaves little doubt in his or anyone's mind that the United States in 1962 is a nation of vast wealth, power, and responsibility.

He turns right down a third-floor hallway and enters a carpeted reception area that could easily be the entrance to a white shoe, D.C. law firm. A young woman sits behind a large reception desk. An armed guard in civilian clothes stands to the right of the unmarked, wooden double-doors just beyond the receptionist's desk.

Before Nick can get to the desk, he is greeted by the receptionist.

"Good morning, Mr. Temple. Mr. Johnson is expecting you."

Nick is impressed: she's efficient and cordial without being familiar. She reaches under her desk and pushes a button. A slight buzz emits from the set of doors. The armed guard opens the right door and Nick walks into one of the many sections of the vast intelligence-gathering nerve center that is the Central Intelligence Agency.

"Let's go see the Old Man."

Nick Temple and Bill Johnson walk out of Johnson's office. They revert to personal chit-chat on their way to see the Director.

"How's Peggy?"

"Never better. She loves my new job. Home by six o'clock most days. Time to spend with her. No more running around dodging bullets and killing Commies."

"She deserves a break."

"What about Ellie and the kids?"

"Not a lot of contact. They're not kids anymore. They're both out of college. I get occasional updates, and that's about it. So far as I can tell, she's still making a nuisance of herself in Pasadena."

"Everyone's healthy?"

"They seem to be."

"Glad to hear it. Here we are. After you, Nick."

←—↔↔↔↔↔↔↔—→

"You look good, Nick."

"Amazing what six weeks in the tropics will do, sir."

"You got pretty damn lucky with that Jeep."

"Guess it just wasn't my time. Tough break for the car thief."

"You play with fire, you're gonna get burned."

"To a crisp," Johnson adds.

The three men share a laugh before the Director brings them back to business.

"We've got you on a flight to Cairo tomorrow. Ridgely's cleared the local national who's going to help us out in Kenya."

"That was quick."

"The Brits gave us their file on her. She had a mid-level clearance already. You'll meet with Ridgely first. He's got a line on the German in Mombasa. If he comes through Cairo, we might be able to grab him. If not, we still need to find out what happened in Voi. Should be a straightforward assignment for someone with her skills."

"Her?"

"Didn't Bill tell you?"

Nick looks at Bill who shrugs his shoulders.

"Anyone tell her what happens to women who work with me?"

"Not yet. We'll leave that to your discretion. Hopefully by then she'll already be committed. Bill's got the file. You can read it on the hop across the pond."

"Not to worry, Nick. No chance you'll fall for this one."

"Not my type?"

"Actually, she's exactly your type. Smart, independent, and easy on the eyes."

"So what's the reason I won't fall for her?"

"None at all. Just wishful thinking on my part."

The Director stands up signaling the end of the brief meeting.

"I've told Ridgely to keep us informed. He's your first and last point of contact over there. If you think it's going to take more than a week to get what we need, stay another week, but that's it. Things have calmed down a bit, but the country's still not stable. No sense pressing your luck. Stay in Mombasa while she's in the field. If you . . ."

Nick cuts him off.

"I think I can handle it, sir."

"Right, sorry. Old habits, I suppose. No offense."

"None taken."

"Good luck then. I hope there's nothing to it, but all of my instincts tell me otherwise."

Nick and the Director shake hands. Bill Johnson and Nick leave the Director's office. They walk silently back to Johnson's office until Nick speaks up.

"Mika, Vanessa, and what's this one's name?"

"Dalila."

"A beautiful name. And a damned shame."

"It's not going to be like that, Nick."

"I hope you're right, my friend. I just hope you're right."

CHAPTER 17

SOME EXPLAINING TO DO

Ulrich Hartmann knew he was in trouble the moment he was not-so-subtly threatened by the King's African Rifles captain on the road from Mombasa to Voi. Taking the captain's malevolent advice and returning to Mombasa meant that he would likely return from Kenya empty handed, a prospect he has been trying desperately to avoid.

Once back in Mombasa, he spent nearly 24 hours straight attempting to make some sort of contact with his countrymen. He tried, without any success, to raise them on the supremely unreliable telephone system; he sent half a dozen cables to their various known haunts in Voi; he made a number of discreet inquiries in the city's European quarter; and he wasted 100 American dollars on a local courier who, after agreeing to deliver Hartmann's urgent message to Voi at the first opportunity, tossed Hartmann's sealed envelope in the nearest waste bin and treated himself and six friends to an extravagant evening out all courtesy of Ulrich Hartmann's expense account.

He plans to spend one more day of searching, calling, and bribing, hoping to catch some tidbit of positive news that he can take back to Moscow with him. One more day alone in Mombasa.

At precisely 7 a.m., he heads out of his room on the second story of the Castle Royal Hotel, down the hotel's elegant staircase, and into the lobby. He exchanges a half-shilling for a copy of *The Daily Nation* at the reception desk and walks to the main dining room on the same floor. The dining room is already busy serving breakfast to the hotel's guests.

Hartmann seats himself, and a waiter immediately brings a cup of hot tea. Hartmann waves him off.

"Coffee," he officiously instructs.

"Of course," the waiter responds and backs away.

Hartmann unfolds his paper, and what he reads nearly causes him to drop in a dead faint. His coffee comes and the waiter asks if Hartmann would like to order breakfast. Hartmann is so engrossed in the story about the two mutilated foreigners found outside of Voi that he doesn't hear the question. The waiter discreetly retreats.

Hartmann reads the article a second and a third time. Moments ago he felt ready to take on the day. Now he is already exhausted and in a state of near panic. He takes a moment to gather himself. He wipes the sweat from his brow with his handkerchief, tosses a few shillings from his jacket pocket on the table, folds the paper, tucks it under his arm, slowly stands up, and nearly sprints out of the dining room. He makes a beeline for the concierge in the hotel's lobby.

The concierge looks up in alarm at the profusely sweating Hartmann.

"How may I be of assistance, sir?"

"I need a ticket on the first flight to Cairo."

CHAPTER 18

TEMPLE ON THE NILE

Hugh Ridgely is an ex-pat. Although his degree in economics, which he took from Cambridge in 1938, is the foundation upon which he built a lucrative career in the American oil industry, it was his almost whimsical decision to study Arabic while at Cambridge, one his father thought frankly foolish, that made such a career possible. After taking his degree he headed straight for America and immediately landed a job with Caltex, the American oil company running around the Arabian Peninsula's east coast in the 1930s hoping to find oil. They found it in bunches, and by 1955 Ridgely's personal fortune was sufficient to allow him to retire at the age of 40. He bought a home on Long Island in the Hamptons and began to settle in for a life of leisure: golf, sailing, occasional trips into New York to take in a Broadway play, and not much else. Within six months he was bored nearly out of his mind.

The Suez Crisis of 1956 was the spark that lit the flame that became Hugh Ridgely's second life. Through a contact from his days at Caltex's eventual successor entity, Aramco, he offered up his knowledge of the Middle East's economy and culture to the American State Department. State referred him to the CIA and within a month he found himself wandering the streets of Cairo helping keep tabs on a growing Soviet presence in Egyptian internal politics. By 1962 the Cairo station was his, and his dream of being a country gentleman relaxing on his estate fronting the Atlantic Ocean was a distant memory.

Ridgely finishes his morning routine of tea, toast and *The Egyptian Gazette* just as his secretary knocks on his door and enters.

"Mr. Temple to see you, sir."

Ridgely wipes his mouth with his napkin.

"Right. Send him right in."

"Mr. Temple, won't you come in?"

Ridgely's secretary opens the door to his office all of the way to allow Nick in the room. Ridgely stands to greet him.

"I say, Temple. Good to see you. Good to see you."

They shake hands.

"Please, have a seat. Have you had a spot of breakfast?"

Nick is mindful of Ridgely's reputation for maintaining his British demeanor in spite of more than 20 years of living abroad.

"I have, thanks, at the hotel," Nick responds as he sits.

"The Victoria?"

"As you suggested."

"I say, you're looking fit, what?"

"Fresh off an extended vacation. Spent some time on St. Thomas in the USVI. Ever been there?"

"Indeed I have. An old chum of mine from Aramco bought a chunk of property after retiring, built a few houses, and now lives the life of a semi-retired landlord. Put me up for a month a few years back. Doesn't even put on shoes most days."

"Sounds like the life."

"Right you are. Now, let's get right down to brass tacks, shall we, Temple?"

Nick nods.

Ridgely sits at his desk and picks up a manila folder.

"You've seen this, I take it."

"I have a copy."

"She's remarkable. Shall I ask her to join us? She's waiting just upstairs."

"By all means."

Ridgely hits a button on his desk intercom.

"Laura, would you have Miss Atieno join us?"

"Straight away," is the response.

Ridgely leans back in his chair.

"Now, what do you suppose the Jerries are up to in East Africa?"

"It's not the Germans that worry me."

"Right you are. The Sovs would love to get their bear claws into another ex-colony. You think that's the game?"

"That makes sense. But at this point, I have no idea."

Ridgely's secretary knocks on the door.

"Do come in."

The door opens and in walks Dalila Atieno, tall, slender, composed without being cold, naturally graceful, and free of pretense.

Nick and Ridgely stand up.

"Nick Temple, this is Dalila Atieno."

Nick and Dalila shake hands formally.

"So happy to meet you, Mr. Temple."

"Likewise," is Nick's clipped response.

"Please, won't you have a seat?"

Dalila takes the chair next to Nick.

"What is it about this awful work that attracts beautiful women?" Nick thinks to himself.

Before Nick can compose himself, Ridgely's desk phone rings.

"Excuse me," he says as he picks up the receiver.

"Ridgely here. . . . Right. . . . When? . . . You're quite certain? . . . Nicely done."

Ridgely hangs up and stands up.

"Looks like we've got to get to work. A local national has spotted our German from Mombasa. He's staying at your hotel. Convenient, what? We'll take my car. I'll fill the two of you in on the way."

The three of them stride out of Hugh Ridgely's unassuming office heading straight for the streets of Cairo.

CHAPTER 19

KNOW WHEN TO FOLD 'EM

Ulrich Hartmann steps from the Victoria Hotel into the rising heat of the late morning. His instructions from Moscow are clear: he is to wait in Cairo. The thought that he may be ordered back to Kenya is almost too much to bear. His hasty exit from Mombasa obviously displeases the powers that be, but the shocking news from Voi convinced him that his was likely the next life to be lost in this Cold War struggle.

"That's him," Ridgely says as he points to a man in tropical whites speaking with the doorman.

Hartmann is trying to get a taxi to take him to the Pyramids west of Giza. He was going to stay in his room until told when to move, but he instead opted to be out in public, convinced he is safer in a crowd than alone behind a single deadbolt.

"Let's grab him, shall we?"

Nick and Dalila scan the crowd as Ridgely pulls up and parks his Land Rover on El Gomhoria across from the hotel's entrance.

"There's a Kenyan coming his way," Dalila points to a man in a khaki suit 50 meters up the street on the hotel side approaching the hotel at a brisk pace.

"He's coming for our man. Let's see if we can't stop him. He's no use to us dead."

The three jump out of the parked car. The busy street is no match for the cool confidence of Dalila Atieno. Looking for all the world like a model at the House of Chanel, she calmly strides through traffic and somehow manages to avoid being crushed in the bargain. Nick sprints towards the hotel entrance, dodging motorbikes, cars, and lorries while keeping his eyes on the rapidly approaching Kenyan, hoping to intercept him.

The Kenyan, now no more than 15 meters from Hartmann, stops abruptly. In a single motion he pulls a Browning Hi-Power semiautomatic pistol from a shoulder holster under his suit jacket and drops to his right knee, instantly assuming a firing position.

"This guy knows what he's doing," Nick thinks to himself as he draws his Beretta. Without breaking stride he fires a single round at the Kenyan. The round slams into the Kenyan's left thigh, precisely as aimed. Remarkably, the wounded assassin barely flinches. Nick squeezes off another round just as the Kenyan fires at Hartmann.

Hartmann, a bullet lodged in his brain, drops face first to the sidewalk the moment Dalila and Ridgely reach the curb. Ridgely reflexively draws his sidearm from his shoulder holster. The two of them immediately stop and turn, dodging traffic to get back to Ridgely's Land Rover. Nick, ten meters farther up the street, does the same, turning away from the Kenyan whose lifeless body is sprawled on the hot Cairo sidewalk, his last mission in life an unqualified success.

CHAPTER 20

REASSESS AND REGROUP

Kasparanov knew the meeting would be at least uncomfortable when he was summoned. Alexander Proykiev, the Deputy Commissar of the KGB's First Chief Directorate, is well-known in the upper echelons of the Soviet intelligence apparatus for his ruthless and often deadly approach to furthering his own career. But Kasparanov remains calm during the interrogation. Having secured the blessing of the General Secretary makes him as close to invulnerable as one can get in the Soviet Union.

"It was a Kenyan. Cairo won't release the body, but it was undoubtedly a Kenyan," Kasparanov points out once again.

"But the reports put the CIA at the scene. There's no question. CIA. What do you suppose the CIA is doing in the middle of a murder of a German national on the streets of Cairo? Do you think it's merely a coincidence?"

Kasparanov takes a drag from his cigarette, puts it out in the ashtray on Proykiev's desk, and responds.

"There is no surveillance. There are only inconclusive statements."

"Should I read it to you once again?" Proykiev thunders. "Someone killed the Kenyan. Are you forgetting? A white man, who left in a late model Land Rover with a white male and an African female. KGB confirmed the American Station Chief in Cairo drives such a car. We don't need surveillance. We don't need photographs. I tell you, the CIA is closing in on your fantastic gamble."

"They know nothing."

"They knew who Hartmann was."

"And where are they now? Leipzig? No. St. Thomas? No. The CIA knows nothing. And if the CIA was in Cairo, Hartmann's in no position to provide them with anything."

"We don't know who the others were or where they are. Only Ridgely, the Station Chief. And he's still in Cairo. For all we know, they may have taken the first flight from Cairo to Leipzig on their way to St. Thomas!"

"Of course they didn't. We can proceed. Even if they get to Voi, what will they find out? Some German medical experiments went badly. It's a familiar story, an old story, and that's why it's a good story, and that's why they have nothing."

Kasparanov hides his fear of this man's power well. He knows he must tread a fine line between confidence and arrogance, that Proykiev will crush him for sport if he senses that Kasparanov's attitude has become dismissive.

"And Schnelling?"

"The formula's complete. It's been tested. The trials were sufficiently conclusive. Now it's a matter of production in a quantity sufficient for the initial attack."

"We should increase his security detail."

"He prefers to work alone."

"He can go to the devil! His preferences at this point are of no concern of mine. His work must be protected. What of the formula?"

"We don't have it yet. I understand our interest in having it, but we must proceed cautiously. He's the only one who knows it, the only one who has it."

"I'll leave that to you, but we have to have the formula. We need security, for him and for us."

"We can't load up St. Thomas with KGB. That will surely get the Americans' attention. It is, after all, their island."

"If nothing else, I concede you are right about that. One man should do it, and I know just the man for the job. Driven, ruthless, a devout killer. He'll be as effective as half a dozen men."

As Proykiev picks up his phone and waits, Kasparanov breathes a barely audible sigh of relief. He has managed to survive another round, and he didn't have to fall back on the General Secretary's considerable clout to do so. He listens as Proykiev instructs his secretary.

"Lyudmila. Bring me the file of Nikolai Gregorovich Kropotkin."

CHAPTER 21

FIRST MISSION

Dalila Atieno cruises easily through the checkpoint that proved so portentous for Ulrich Hartmann. As she continues on to Voi she muses over the sudden turn her life has taken. One moment she is a rather anonymous clerk who eagerly anticipates the full transition to independence in store for Kenya. That anticipation makes her no different from most of her countrymen. While her desire to enter politics once the transition is complete is almost part of her DNA, she never considered doing much more than the routine work she's been engaged in at the Provincial Commissioner's office until that moment. And then came the request from Rodgers.

Since then she has been given access to classified information she could have gone to prison for possessing a week earlier; she has been introduced to Hugh Ridgely, the American CIA Station Chief for Cairo, and Nick Temple, another CIA agent; and she witnessed two nearly simultaneous and very public killings that are apparently tied to her new career, if one can call it that, no more than ten minutes later.

Temple's explanation of why the death of the German, which initially was of no concern to her, was more significant than the death of the Kenyan helps her focus on what may be at stake as she navigates her way through the recent turn of events on the road to Voi.

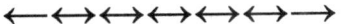

"Show me."

The boy takes her hand and leads her down the road.

"When did you find them?"

"In the morning. I was walking to school."

"Who did you tell?"

"My mother and father. Straight away. I ran home and told them. I didn't touch anything. I told the policeman that."

"Did you know them?"

"No, ma'am. But I could see they were dead. Right there."

He stops, and letting go of her hand points to the roadside ditch, its grass and weeds still matted from the weight of the dead men's mutilated bodies.

As Dalila looks at the ditch a patrol car pulls up. Behind the wheel is the same policeman who called in the boy's discovery of the two bodies. He gets out of his car and walks over to Dalila and the boy.

"Good morning."

"Good morning, officer," Dalila responds.

"What brings you out here this morning?"

Dalila sees no need to conceal her identity. At the same time she sees no need to provide a full accounting. The officer strikes her immediately as capable and smart, just from his carriage and bearing. Being as honest as she can be seems the most prudent course of action.

"My name is Dalila Atieno. I work for the Provincial Commissioner's Office in Nairobi. They've taken an interest in the case, and asked me to look into it."

"How can I assist you, Miss Atieno?"

"It's simple, really. Why were they killed?"

The officer turns to the young boy and puts his arm on his shoulder.

"You'll be just in time for school if you hurry."

"Yes, sir."

The lad scampers off. The officer watches after him and then returns his attention to Dalila.

"I can tell you what the people here in Voi believe, but our department has not been able to confirm any of this."

"If you don't mind."

"Not at all. The two men came to Voi about a year ago. One called himself a doctor. The other was his assistant. They set up a small medical clinic in the heart of town and began receiving patients."

"That seems a bit odd, don't you think."

"They connected themselves to a Lutheran missionary. It was a loose connection, but the fact that they offered medical services made their presence welcome and kept the questions to a minimum."

"Until what?"

"Until about a month ago. Two young girls, both teenagers, and a teenaged boy were treated by them. They came in for tetanus shots, and within days all three had developed polio. The boy died when it attacked his lungs, and the two girls are now unable to walk."

"How do they know these men were to blame?"

"They don't. And it's actually quite fantastic. All of the young people in this area receive the polio vaccine as a condition of attending school. I think the wrong men have been blamed and executed. Perhaps a defective vaccine is to blame. But I honestly do not know at this point."

"Any suspects?"

"None. It was made to look like a Mau Mau killing, but I don't believe it. That's just a cover. Whoever did this was not interested in politics. They were interested in revenge."

Dalila has heard enough.

"Thank you so much for your time, officer."

"Do you need a lift?"

"No, thank you. My car is just down the road, in front of the boy's family's house."

"How did you find him?"

"It wasn't hard. Plenty of talk at the market yesterday led me to him. It's amazing what one can find out when one asks the right people."

"Indeed it is."

"Good day, then."

Dalila offers her hand. They shake hands formally.

"Good day to you, ma'am."

She turns and walks back towards her car parked no more than two blocks away. The officer, convinced that Miss Dalila Atieno does more than simply work for the Provincial Commissioner, adds her appearance in Voi to the growing list of questions surrounding the brutal murder of the two German "doctors."

CHAPTER 22

CONNECTING SOME DOTS

Low tea at Mombasa's Castle Royal Hotel was Ridgely's idea. Dalila seems in her element, but Nick could use a frosty schooner of draft beer. He has been leaving the debriefing to Ridgely.

"You're certain they sought tetanus boosters?"

"There was no deviation in any of the conversations I had on that essential point."

"Is it possible that a defective tetanus booster can induce the same symptoms as polio?"

None of the three says a word until Nick finally speaks up.

"That should be easy enough to determine. I'll get the folks at Langley working on it. I think it's fair to assume in the meantime that someone has found a way to administer a strain of polio to individuals, and it appears that the strain is resistant to the existing polio vaccine."

"That was my conclusion," Dalila offers.

"You should have said as much," Ridgely scolds.

Nick jumps in.

"He's right. You're on this team for a number of reasons, one of which is your brain. It's imperative that you speak your mind, particularly when it involves any sort of analysis."

"That will take some getting used to."

"You'd better get used to it in a hurry."

Nick is well aware of the fact that it is almost unheard of in 1962 for two white men, one an American, the other a British expat, to look to an African woman for much of anything other than perhaps answering a phone, typing a few letters, and making coffee or tea. And he understands that Dalila's reticence to speak up stems from decades or more of relentless conditioning. But more than anything else he knows that team members in his line of work have to be absolutely forthcoming irrespective of sex, skin color, or national origin, that once you're on the team, once you're in the game, you're in all the way.

Ridgely finishes his tea, wipes his mouth with his napkin, looks at his watch, and gets up from the table.

"Look, you two. I've got to get back to Cairo. There's a flight leaving in two hours. My job was to put you in touch with each other, not to roam about Mombasa hoping God knows what turns up."

"We'll take the same flight and catch a hop to the States from Cairo. I'll need to send some messages from your office so they can be looking into what Dalila found in Voi while we're en route. Can we do that tonight after we land?"

"I'm at your service."

Nick turns to Dalila.

"Have you been to the States?"

"You'd know if you'd actually read my file."

Nick can't help smiling at her assertiveness. She's a quick study, no doubt about it.

"That's more like it. Hugh, can you get a visa for her?"

"In a heartbeat. First order of business tomorrow in the a.m. I'll see the two of you at the airport."

Ridgely turns and leaves.

As soon as Ridgely is out of earshot, Nick looks to Dalila.

"Before you make this trip, I need to make sure you know what you may be getting yourself into."

"More of what happened in Cairo?"

"Cairo was a taste, and not much more."

"Are you trying to scare me away?"

"No."

"What, then?"

"I want to be able to tell myself that you understood the risks; that you entered into this awful line of work with your eyes wide open."

"You can tell yourself that now, if you feel the need."

"It's not now I'm talking about."

"When exactly are we talking about, if you don't mind my asking?"

"When I'm asked to identify your body."

CHAPTER 23

PLANTING THE SEED

"The goal is to be fully operational by October. The sleeper cells will be alerted and can be activated on less than 24-hours' notice. That leaves the question of the diversion."

The General Secretary has listened patiently to the briefing of young Yevgeny Kasparanov. Indeed, he let his mind wander at times. The details Kasparanov has been providing have been on his desk for some time now, a pleasing result of a pervasive if at times clumsy internal security apparatus. Kasparanov's diversion plan is another matter. With the exception of recordings of Kasparanov's charming, innocuous conversations with his wife, the General Secretary has no advance information on what this section of the briefing will reveal. He sharpens his focus as the young man continues.

"Simply stated, I propose that the Soviet Union deliver for immediate operational posture a strategically significant number of intermediate range missiles armed with nuclear warheads to Cuba."

Kasparanov pauses. He can see he has the full attention of the General Secretary, so he continues.

"Such a delivery will undoubtedly consume the attention of America's military complex, its civilian and military intelligence agencies, and its political leadership at all levels of government. They will have no choice, due to domestic and international political pressure, to call on all of their resources to manage the widest range of potential responses to the existential threat posed by the delivery, installation, and activation of these weapons of mass destruction. At that moment, using the missiles as a highly credible diversion, we can with relative ease and with little chance of detection or apprehension, insert via simple pressurized containers into six metropolitan areas the reengineered strain for maximum effect with minimum risk, expense, and effort."

The General Secretary sits silently for a moment. He glances at the map on his office wall. He stares at Kasparanov for what seems to the young man like an eternity. Kasparanov, who can feel his heartbeat in his throat, knows this moment is the most important one in his career, perhaps his life. Finally, the General Secretary speaks.

"You have found a thorn, perhaps the most deadly of thorns, and you have found a way to twist that thorn, and to focus all of the Americans' attention on the pain caused by that thorn. Your solution is brilliant. I'll relay your briefing to our military commanders. They will balk initially, but you can consider your plan approved. You are to remain at all times available. No detail can be overlooked. You will work on nothing else until the moment of deployment of both mission and diversion. I will see to it that you are undisturbed."

"Thank you for your confidence. I will do my utmost to demonstrate it is not misplaced."

"I know you will. If this plan of yours fails, we'll both be looking for work, or for our heads!"

Kasparanov shudders at the mental image of two decapitated men wandering aimlessly, searching for their severed heads, one of which is his.

CHAPTER 24

HELP UNWANTED

A de Havilland Canada DHC-3 Otter lands gracefully on the brilliant blue and green water in the harbor of Charlotte Amalie. It taxis on its floats toward the seaplane base west of downtown. Its floats are equipped with wheels for amphibious use allowing the aircraft to seamlessly climb the concrete pad leading out of the harbor to the base.

The Otter comes to a complete stop on level concrete shortly after leaving the water. As the pilot cuts the engine an attendant hustles to the aircraft, chocks the wheels, and opens the fuselage door aft of the seaplane's overhead wing. Unfolding his considerable frame as he extracts himself from the cramped compartment, the aircraft's lone passenger steps into the midday heat of St. Thomas in August. The passenger looks displeased, the result of a permanent scowl etched by a bullet during a wild chase through the streets of Berlin four years ago. The attendant cautiously approaches the malevolent looking passenger with a single piece of luggage.

"What are you doing with that?" the passenger bellows as he rips the bag from the attendant's hand.

The passenger chuckles mildly to himself as the attendant scurries away. He removes his aviator sunglasses and wipes his brow with his handkerchief. He checks his watch and puts his sunglasses back on just as a late model hardtop Toyota Land Cruiser pulls up and comes to a skidding stop inches from him.

The driver opens the passenger door from the inside, jumps out of the car, grabs the passenger's suitcase and tosses it in the back of the Land Cruiser. By the time he's back in the driver's seat, the passenger has already seated himself and closed his door.

"You're late. Why do you wait? Drive!" he commands.

"Of course."

And with that, Nikolai Gregorovich Kropotkin, the man whose malignant heart bears more hatred for Nick Temple than for any other man on the planet, extends the growing reach of the Soviet Union deep into the American Paradise.

CHAPTER 25

JUST THE FACTS

Dr. Peter Hall, professor of microbiology at Johns Hopkins University, is impressed by the modern, sprawling complex his tax dollars helped build. It isn't every day that outsiders get a glimpse into the insular world of America's intelligence efforts, so when he was invited to discuss unspecified matters with the Director of Central Intelligence he jumped at the opportunity. He probably should have worn a tie, but he didn't want to appear too much the academic. Just as he glances at his watch and notices that it is exactly 10 a.m., the Director's secretary approaches him.

"Dr. Hall?"

He stands.

"In the flesh."

"Thank you so much for coming this morning. The Director is ready to see you. Will you come with me?"

The 38 year-old Hall is also impressed by the Director's punctuality.

"Lead the way."

He is led to a large set of wooden double doors. The Director's secretary knocks and opens one of the doors without waiting for an answer.

"Dr. Hall is here, sir."

The Director gets up from his desk and comes around to greet his guest as Dr. Hall enters the spacious office.

"Thank you, Cheryl. Dr. Hall, thanks for coming this morning."

The two men shake hands.

"Let me introduce you. This is Nick Temple. Nick was our Station Chief in Berlin for many years. His specialty is the Soviet Union and East Germany, but we let him roam fairly far afield these days."

"Nice to meet you, Nick."

"My pleasure, Dr. Hall."

"Please, call me Pete. It's what my seven brothers and sisters call me, so I'm kind of used to it."

"This is Dalila Atieno. She's on loan to us from what remains of the British government in Kenya. Studied economics and politics at the University of London. She's helping us on the matter we've asked you to consult on."

"Miss Atieno."

"If you insist on calling me Miss Atieno, I'm afraid I will have to call you Dr. Hall."

"Fair enough. I'll go with Dalila if you'll stick with Pete."

"Agreed."

"And these two gentlemen are rarely far behind when Nick's working on something: Kyle Richardson and Bill Johnson, both long time Soviet watchers."

"Kyle, Bill, nice to meet the two of you."

Handshakes all around.

"Now, let's get down to business, shall we?"

The Director leads them all to a solid cherry, oval conference table on the right hand side of his vast office. The table has room for ten. Once everyone is seated, the Director begins.

"Nick, how about a quick rundown to give Pete an idea of what we're talking about here."

"Sure. Well, it's simple, really. A few weeks back a Kenyan drove a car filled with TNT into a café in Mombasa. The car contained, in addition to the explosives, a Soviet cultural attaché. The attaché was supposed to meet an East German national at the café. We're fairly certain they were going to drive to a small city in the Kenyan interior called Voi. Are you at all familiar with Kenya?"

"Sorry to say, but I'm not."

"No need to apologize. With the exception of Dalila, the rest of us are getting our sea legs, as it were. At any rate, the German never made it to Voi. Had he made it, he would have discovered that two of his countrymen, a physician and his assistant, had been murdered, disemboweled, and thrown into a ditch. I'll let Dalila take it from here."

Dalila straightens up. Her poise is phenomenal considering the circumstances she currently finds herself in.

"I traveled to Voi to speak with the locals. The two Germans had been operating a medical clinic for some time and had come to be trusted and accepted by the local population. Recently, three different patients–a young man and two teenaged girls–were given tetanus boosters at that clinic. All three almost immediately developed symptoms of polio. The young man died from complications of the disease, and the two girls are both wheelchair-bound, the muscles in their lower extremities having been targeted by the disease."

Dr. Hall interrupts.

"Do you think these men are deliberately injecting patients with poliomyelitis?"

Nick jumps in.

"It's only slightly more complicated than that. Dalila?"

"All three of the victims received the polio vaccine at least four years ago."

"Ah, a defective vaccine," Dr. Hall muses.

Dalila is quick to respond.

"There is no indication from anyone else in the potentially affected population that the vaccine these three received was defective. The affected population would statistically be much larger if a defective vaccine had been administered. A total of three cases is not statistically significant. We have, therefore, rejected the defective vaccine hypothesis."

The room is silent. All eyes are on Dr. Hall. He is deep in thought. He removes his wire-rimmed glasses, cleans them with his handkerchief, and puts them back on. He carefully folds his handkerchief before he stuffs it into the breast pocket of his sport coat. He leans forward on his elbows and addresses the Director.

"You want to know if it's possible to engineer a strain of poliomyelitis that is resistant to the current vaccine."

He glances about for confirmation which he gets from several slight nods.

He takes a deep breath and measures his words carefully.

"Well, the answer of course is yes."

"Damn," is the Director's response as he pounds his fist on the conference table.

CHAPTER 26

CHANGE OF PLANS

Bill Johnson's suburban Alexandria home is everything his wife Peggy has ever wanted: split level, three bedrooms, two-and-a-half baths, a nice patio out back for cookouts when the Virginia summers permit, and a spacious backyard that completes the picture of her family's solid, modest success.

The day promised to be hot and muggy, typical for late August, but a front pushed through earlier in the afternoon, and the evening air is unseasonably cool and dry, perfect for enjoying dinner outdoors. Bill and Peggy's guests are Kyle Richardson and his wife Carolyn, who is six months pregnant with their first child, their old friend Nick Temple, and the newest member of Nick's team, Dalila Atieno. Bill flips steaks on his grill and works on a can of beer; the other members of team Temple talk about their meeting earlier in the day with Dr. Hall as they nurse various mixed drinks.

Peggy and Carolyn busy themselves in the kitchen on the other side of a sliding glass door. Peggy puts together a large bowl of potato salad and starts boiling a pot of water for several ears of corn on the cob. Carolyn walks outside, grabs an empty iced tea pitcher from the patio table, gives her husband a kiss on the cheek, and goes back into the kitchen.

"When is your baby due?" Dalila asks Kyle.

"November 11th, but they say the first one is always late."

"You'll send me a picture?"

"If you're not still in D.C. Absolutely."

"I'm heading home to Nairobi at the end of the week, unless Nick thinks I should stay."

"I'm not sure what we've got at this point. Without anything more, the trail is pretty damn cold. One dead Russian, three dead Germans, a dead Kenyan, three cases of polio, and a wild theory are about all we have at this point. Maybe you can scare up a few more bits of info back in Kenya. Otherwise, I'm fresh out of ideas on this one."

"Wouldn't be the first time we've had to wait for something to come our way," Kyle offers.

The front doorbell rings. Peggy wipes her hands on her apron and heads out of the kitchen to answer the door. She opens it and the Director, an 8 1/2 x 11 manila envelope in one hand and a bottle of 1958 Barbaresco Bertolino in the other, greets her.

"Peggy, how are you?"

"I'm fine. Come in, come in. You're late," she teases.

He steps inside and the two of them walk towards the kitchen.

"It's the strangest thing. I seem to be in charge of everything but my own schedule. What's cooking?"

"Bill's got the steaks going out back. Why don't you join them? Want me to open that?"

"That's what it's for."

He hands the bottle to her as they enter the kitchen.

"Carolyn. How are you?"

"I'm fine, sir. How are you?"

"No complaints. The old man out back?"

"They all are. See if you can't get them to stop talking shop."

The Director holds up the envelope.

"Not much chance of that, I'm afraid."

He heads out back as the two women return to preparing dinner.

"We were just talking about you," Nick says as he greets his boss.

"Dalila, you have to learn not to pay attention to these men. They rarely tell the truth, especially when they're talking about me."

"I'll consider myself warned, sir."

"Actually, we were just discussing the dead end we've come to on this Kenya affair."

"I might be able to help. This came in last night."

The Director takes a 5 x 7 black and white photograph out of the envelope. He throws the picture on the picnic table.

Nick immediately recognizes the man who tortured him for what seemed like an eternity four years ago in East Berlin.

"Kropotkin. Where did that pig surface?"

"You're not going to believe it."

"Nothing that guy does will surprise me."

"A freelancer saw him board a plane for London at Belgrade International. We alerted London, and from there he headed to Miami en route to Puerto Rico. He cleared customs in San Juan using a forged Yugoslavian passport. In San Juan he hired a private seaplane for the short hop to Charlotte Amalie. The report hit my desk right before I left the office. As far as we know, he's still on the island."

They're all silent, looking at Nick, waiting for a reaction.

Nick exhales.

"That's good work."

"Indeed it is, with a little luck," the Director agrees.

"We can forget about Nairobi. We're going to St. Thomas. Kropotkin's a dead giveaway. Our German professor has got to be working for the Sovs. It's too much of a coincidence. We have to find out what he's doing."

"My thoughts exactly, but I have no authority to order Dalila to make the trip."

"I've always wanted to visit the West Indies," Dalila says through a radiant smile sent Nick's way.

"It's settled then. Get in touch with Pete Hall. See if he can go with you. You might need his scientific expertise if you stumble across something."

"Good idea. Let's hope his teaching load will permit a bit of field work."

"Kyle, I want you to go along. Given the one attempt on Nick's life, he may need some additional muscle. When's Carolyn due?"

"Early November."

"You should be back well before then. This trip is probably nothing more than recon. We've got to see if we can connect the dots."

"Not to worry. She knows the drill."

"You're going to need to requisition some equipment. Bill, you follow up and make sure they get whatever they need. It's going to have to follow you down there to keep the operation low key."

Nick turns to Bill Johnson who is diligently working the grill.

"I'll call you first thing in the morning, Bill."

"Enough with Kropotkin. Steaks are ready. Time to eat," Bill announces as he loads them onto a platter.

"I'll help the ladies," Dalila says as she turns to head for the kitchen.

Bill stops her.

"Not a chance. You're our guest. Kyle, you're on K.P., buddy."

Richardson sets his highball glass on the patio table.

"It's like I never left the Corps."

The men laugh lightly.

Kyle Richardson heads towards the kitchen knowing he has to tell his pregnant wife he's heading back into the field, knowing he can't tell her where he's going, and knowing he can't tell her when he's coming back. He knows what she can't: he's heading straight for a man who spent the better part of an hour a few years back trying to kill Nick Temple, Bill Johnson, and Kyle Richardson.

CHAPTER 27

WITH FRIENDS LIKE THIS

Professor Hartmut Schnelling is appalled by the hulking presence of the malevolent Kropotkin. He resolves to send an encrypted cable at the first opportunity demanding the recall of the crude thug. In the meantime he knows he must do his best to placate the Slavic beast while revealing as little as possible about his work. He knows that Kropotkin's sudden appearance on the island likely signals Moscow's intention to shove him aside now that the formula has been successfully tested. And he knows that a shove from a creature like Kropotkin is likely to be a deadly shove into an early grave.

"You really should do that in the backroom if you insist on doing it in my house."

Kropotkin ignores the professor and continues to clean his 9mm Makarov.

"Is your hotel room satisfactory?"

Kropotkin stops and looks up at Schnelling.

"It doesn't concern you. The only thing I want to hear from you is when you'll take me to your lab."

Schnelling works hard to maintain his composure and to keep his voice steady, even cordial.

"We can't just drive out there, you must understand. You're probably being watched. You practically announced your arrival with your behavior at the harbor, so it is imperative that we wait some decent interval before we risk being seen together. I should think that a spy would be a bit more subtle."

Kropotkin laughs. He puts the pistol back together and, without looking up from his work, addresses his host.

"Spy? You think I am spy? I spit on dead bodies of spies after killing them with my bare hands."

Schnelling shivers with disgust. To calm his nerves he lights a cigarette and retreats to his kitchen. As he thinks about the injustice of having to kowtow to a monster like Kropotkin he hears the front door open and then slam shut. He walks back into his living room and sees that Kropotkin has left without a word. He takes another drag on his cigarette and exhales. His hand trembles as he puts the cigarette out in an ashtray on his teak and bamboo coffee table. The air smells like the machine oil Kropotkin was using on his Makarov. The smell nauseates Professor Hartmut Schnelling. A man who has perfected a means of silently destroying the lives of millions is suddenly unnerved when faced with the possibility of his own violent demise. He heads to his wall safe to extract the code book that will tell him how to construct his urgent cable to his Russian overlords.

CHAPTER 28

PEERING THROUGH THE CURTAIN

Dr. Kampfried's brother's suspicions began almost immediately. The fact that the authorities cremated the body before any family member could claim it was enough to make anyone question the official cause of death. Why cremate someone who has died of a heart attack? Why not let the family decide how to dispose of the body? His family has been burying their dead in Rostock since the 18th century. And what about his sister-in-law? Her continued disappearance makes the way his brother's death was handled even more mysterious. Now Emile Kampfried waits along the waterfront in Rostock hoping that his pending midnight meeting will provide some answers.

The call came a week ago from a woman claiming to be a nurse where his brother worked at the time of his death. She said she had information she wanted to share, that she couldn't elaborate over the phone. She also demanded that he pay her two thousand West German Deutsche Marks, an enormous sum for anyone living in East Germany. Take it or leave it, she demanded. The meeting was set.

He feels for the envelope in his breast pocket: twenty notes, one hundred Deutsche Marks each. He checks his watch as he hears light footsteps on the cobblestone coming his way. He looks up and out of the fog steps a nondescript, middle-aged woman, the collar of her heavy cloth coat turned up against the night's chill. She walks right up to him.

"Kampfried?"

"Yes."

"Do you have the money?"

"I want to know what I'm buying."

"If you don't have the money, then we're through."

"I have it. What do you have?"

The woman looks around before she starts.

"I was a nurse where your brother worked. I was on duty the day he died."

"A heart attack?"

"Don't be stupid."

"What, then?"

"Are you sure you want to hear this?"

"Go ahead."

"He shot himself. He was at his desk in his office right after finishing his rounds, and he put a bullet in his head."

"Liar!"

"I ran in when I heard the shot. He was dead when I got there. There was nothing I could do. There was a Luger in his hand. It was still smoking. That's how fast I got there."

The mention of the Luger, his brother's prized possession, compels Kampfried to admit to himself that this woman is likely telling the truth.

"Why? Did he leave a note? Did he say anything?"

"Not a thing."

"Was there something at work that would have driven him to it?"

"As I said, he had just finished his rounds. His last patient was a young man with polio. There were rumors."

"What sort of rumors?"

"That your brother was injecting patients with the polio virus. Where's the damn money?"

Kampfried is stunned. He can barely comprehend the horror of what he has just heard about his brother. Slowly, staring blankly at the ground, he pulls the envelope from his pocket. She grabs it from him, turns and quickly disappears.

Kampfried walks in a trance towards his car, a new Trabant 600, parked less than two blocks away. As he grabs the car's door handle he hears a single gunshot break the damp silence of the night.

"STASI!" he thinks to himself. He scrambles into the small car, starts its two-stroke, two-cylinder engine, and quickly drives away, wondering if East Germany's State Security also has a bullet for him.

CHAPTER 29

THE BEST LAID PLANS

Yevgeny Kasparanov hasn't been home in three days. Cloistered like a monk in his small office, two armed guards posted at his door, he pores over volume after volume of the Soviet Union's most closely guarded secrets as well as its most mundane infrastructure details: total throw-weights of all of its deployed nuclear ballistic missiles; precise ranges for each of its medium and intermediate range ballistic missiles; fuel requirements for each type of missile and launcher; optimum activation timelines; gross weights for all launching equipment, including communication, rear echelon, and support systems; average monthly available merchant marine tonnage; average delivery times from Sevastopol and Vladivostok to Havana by week, month, and season; rail connections to Sevastopol and Vladivostok from every conceivable point in the Soviet Union together with available rolling stock at each connecting point; current billeting of all fully-trained missile crews; topographical maps of a variety of potentially suitable launch sites on Cuba; existing communication, road, and rail infrastructure in Cuba; in short, any bit of information needed to plan the insertion into Cuba of a frightening array of nuclear weapons aimed at the heart of the United States.

The information now at his fingertips is being carefully translated by him into a detailed plan of execution. As he works through the logistics of deployment from harbor to launch site in Cuba, he knows he is no more than 24 hours away from the first complete draft of such a plan.

A gentle knock on his door startles him.

"Enter!" he commands with some irritation.

The door opens briskly as the General Secretary enters, his considerable body taking up the last square inches of free space in the cramped room. Kasparanov immediately stands to greet him.

"Forgive me. I had no idea it was you."

"It's of no matter. Please, sit down, Yevgeny Nikolaievitch. I came to see how you're progressing."

Kasparanov sits as ordered.

"Yes. Well, let me see."

Kasparanov pauses and gathers his thoughts and breath before launching into an abrupt overview of his plan.

"It is my recommendation that we immediately insert an advanced team into Cuba to confirm the suitability of the launch sites I have identified. At the same time, given the challenges of infrastructure and current location, we should begin immediate deployment of the necessary personnel and materiel from their current locations. My report, which will be complete by this time tomorrow, details locations, transportation routes and methods, and ports for embarkation to Havana."

"And what will all of this activity achieve?"

"At a minimum, we can complete the delivery of an allocation of R-12 Dvina missiles armed with nuclear warheads by the third week in September, to be fully operational within three weeks of delivery."

"And what of our true objective?"

"All indications are that bulk manufacture is the final component to be completed, ironically, in the so-called American Paradise."

The General Secretary laughs slightly.

"Well then, you will finish your report tomorrow?"

"Yes, sir."

"When you're done, take a day or two off to tend to that beautiful wife of yours. It's not good to leave such a woman sitting at home alone."

"Of course."

"And now I'll leave you to your work."

The General Secretary turns to leave. He opens the door, stops, and turns.

"Is there anything I can get you, my young friend?"

Kasparanov is stunned by the offer. The General Secretary offering to fetch a snack for him! The General Secretary calling him "my young friend!" What a moment! He is almost speechless.

"No, Comrade General Secretary. No, I am fine. I assure you."

"I will have some tea sent up. I'm sure you could use it."

"Thank you so much. I certainly could."

The General Secretary leaves Kasparanov's office and closes the door behind him. He leaves behind a young man almost dizzy with pride, a young man who will now redouble his efforts to rain destruction down on the enemies of the Soviet Union, a young man who harbors no doubts about the rectitude of unleashing a horrific agent of terror on unsuspecting innocent populations across the American landscape.

CHAPTER 30

ISLAND INVASION

Dr. Peter Hall and Dalila Atieno walk separately through the sleek, cool lobby of the sprawling Virgin Isle Hotel overlooking the harbor at Charlotte Amalie. They mix easily with the legions of well-to-do guests of the largest resort on the island. Built in 1950, the hotel was the first modern resort in the U.S. Virgin Islands, and its completion ushered in an era of modern tourism in the American Paradise. The Virgin Isle's mountainside setting takes full advantage not only of the spectacular view of the Caribbean Sea south of the small capital city, but also of the fresh trade winds that routinely caress the Leeward Islands of the Lesser Antilles. A spacious sun deck packed with cushioned chaise lounges surrounding a sparkling oval pool completes a setting more suited to an extended tropical frolic than the deadly serious business of Cold War espionage.

Hall and Atieno add themselves to the small queue forming at the registration desk.

"All courtesy of the American taxpayer," Dalila quips quietly over her shoulder.

"We'll have to make sure they get good value. Besides, we're only here for a week. If we have to stay longer, Nick says he may have less opulent and less visible lodgings for us towards the west end of the island."

Nick and Kyle Richardson checked in last night and left their hotel rooms first thing in the morning to recon a safe house for the four of them.

The Virgin Isle, its constant boisterous crowds providing a degree of security through anonymity, will have to do in the meantime.

Pete Hall looks around as he waits in line to register. The idea of being thrust into the middle of a dangerous contest between the world's premier nuclear powers appeals to his sense of adventure. But as he scans the well-heeled crowd he has to admit he wouldn't be able pick a KGB agent out of a crowd of MI5 operatives, let alone hold his own in the mix if things suddenly heated up. With little to go on besides what he was able to glean from his one appearance at CIA headquarters and the slimmest of briefings from Temple when he was recruited for the trip, he hopes his role is limited to providing scientific expertise rather than firepower or muscle.

Dalila Atieno brings a different set of skills to the team. In the brief time that Nick has worked with her, she has impressed him with her courage, confidence, and intellect. She never flinched during the shootout in Cairo, and she handled herself like a seasoned veteran in Voi. The questions she asked Nick during their layover in San Juan after absorbing the file prepared for her at Langley—questions about timing, assets, local intel, logistics, entry points, hard targets, contingencies, redundancies, and more than a dozen other subjects—revealed a nimble mind perfectly suited to precise and nearly instantaneous analysis. Courageous, confident, and exceedingly bright. Whether she knows it or not, whether she likes it or not, Dalila Atieno is for the moment an American spy.

CHAPTER 31

SINS OF OUR BROTHERS

His nerves are shot. He knows his third cup of coffee in less than an hour isn't likely to help, but the small café along the waterfront in Rostock is his only refuge. He stares at his copy of *Neues Deutschland* as the events of the last 48 hours continue to race through his mind. A middle-aged man in a gray overcoat and black fedora suddenly slides into the only other seat at his small table.

"Guten Morgen, Kampfried."

Kampfried is nearly in a panic. Certain that he is about to feel the full wrath of the DDR's dreaded STASI, he is mute.

The waiter approaches.

"Kaffe, bitte," the stranger orders.

The waiter looks at Kampfried who simply shakes his head to indicate he wants nothing. The waiter departs.

The stranger addresses Kampfried in barely audible English.

"You look like a man who's afraid to go to sleep."

"English! Is this some sort of STASI trick?" Kampfried thinks to himself.

"Ich verstehe nicht."

"Bullshit. You understand every goddam word I'm saying, so you can drop the act."

The waiter returns with the stranger's coffee. The stranger reaches into his overcoat and pulls out an envelope. Kampfried's eyes bulge almost to the point of popping when he recognizes the envelope. He can see it is still full of West German 100 mark notes. The man takes the only East German five mark note from the envelope and hands it to the waiter. The waiter begins to fish for change from a pocket in his apron.

"Trinkgeld."

"Danke."

"Bitte."

The waiter once again departs.

"Here's your money back. She won't be needing it."

The stranger tosses the envelope at Kampfried who, with his hands trembling badly, eventually manages to put it into the breast pocket of his jacket.

"Who are you?"

"A friend. What did she tell you?"

"Did you kill her?"

"Don't be a sap. She was killed by your fucking secret police before I could talk to her."

"Then how did you get the money?"

"Picked it off the body your dedicated public servants left lying on the pavement. Look, you've probably got about 24 hours to live. I can help you, but not if you don't tell me what she told you."

"It was about my brother."

"He shot himself."

"How do you know?"

"We've been watching your brother since the end of the war. He's lucky he wasn't prosecuted at Nürnberg. Now what else did she tell you? You've got ten seconds or I'm out of here and you're on your own."

Kampfried hangs his head in defeat and mumbles, "He was doing some experiments."

"Medical?"

"Yes. Of course. He was a doctor."

"Bullshit, round two. We both know he was a butcher, Emile. What kind of medical experiments?"

"She said he was injecting patients with the polio virus."

"A sick fuck right to the end. I guess a tiger really can't change its stripes."

"What about me?"

"What about you?"

"Can you help me? I just wanted to find out how my brother died."

"You've been living with the Commies since 1945 and you still don't know you're not supposed to ask any questions? I thought you were smarter than that, Emile."

"Can you help me?"

"Sure I can. Tonight. There's a freighter bound for Gdansk, the Nadezhda Krupskaya. Departure from Rostock is 11:30 p.m. local time. Be dockside by 11:15."

"Gdansk? What happens in Gdansk?"

"Nothing. We'll get you off the Krupskaya about two hours out. A launch will take you to Malmø. I'll be on board to make sure you get to Sweden. You just have to stay alive until 11:15 tonight. Think you can handle that?"

The stranger stands. Emile, once again unable to speak, says nothing.

"I guess we'll find out. No suitcases. The clothes on your back and whatever you can stuff in your pockets. You're not coming back."

The stranger, former Berlin freelancer Cliff Thompson, departs leaving Emile Kampfried as terrified as he was in the spring of 1945 when it seemed like the entire Soviet Army was heading straight for Rostock.

CHAPTER 32

THE CAT'S AWAY

Professor Schnelling downshifts his durable 1960 Volvo 210 station wagon as he winds his way towards Santa Maria Bay on the north side of St. Thomas. The ruins of an abandoned 17th century sugar plantation, accessible via the narrow dirt road Schnelling is negotiating, provide the perfect cover for his lab. Most of the materials for the lab, and the crews to construct it, were brought in by water more than two years ago to avoid detection by the locals. Schnelling sold the idea to the young but well-positioned Yevgeny Kasparanov after becoming convinced he could produce a strain of the polio virus resistant to all existing vaccines. He took full advantage of the Soviet Union's desperate and to-date unsuccessful attempts to match America's nuclear arsenal by offering the promise of a physically and psychologically devastating weapon that could be produced and deployed at a tiny fraction of the cost of either nuclear or conventional forces. He relied on Kasparanov to do the rest and he was not disappointed.

The compact but sophisticated laboratory sits on the smallest of rises at the east end of the bay. Dense tropical growth covers the ruins making the lab, built within the walls of the old sugar boiling house, virtually undetectable from the air. In the unlikely event a traveler finds himself on the single, unimproved road leading to the bay, his chances of seeing the lab from the ground are no better. An overgrown footpath leading from the road to the lab more than 50 meters in from the road is the only evidence that anything other than wilderness surrounds Santa Maria Bay.

Schnelling stops at the footpath and gets out of his car. He had always intended to remove the written records of his work from the lab for safekeeping once the formula was perfected, but the sudden appearance of Kropotkin on the island caught him off guard. Since Kropotkin's arrival Schnelling has been living in fear of the threat to his personal safety the theft of his records would represent. He is certain they are his only security; he is also certain that Kropotkin has been ordered to destroy that security by gathering whatever information he can from Schnelling and his lab. He guesses correctly that Kropotkin's preference is to bypass what's on paper in favor of extracting what he can directly from the professor by any means necessary.

The specter of Kropotkin's presence on the island stalks Schnelling as he makes his way through the weeds and ruins to the sanctuary of his workplace. He curses himself for stupidly underestimating the cold brutality of his coconspirators.

CHAPTER 33

ONE STEP BEHIND

Nick Temple sits in a small room on the third floor of Government House in Charlotte Amalie. After several tries, he manages to raise the Director back at Langley.

"Jesus, this is a bad connection."

"One more reason we should set up shop down here. The Government House comms center isn't exactly state of the art."

"It'll have to do for now."

"I got your message, sir. What's going on?"

The Director pauses on the other end before continuing.

"Nick, you remember Cliff Thompson?"

"Absolutely. He was Vanessa's first point of contact. Went missing about a year ago. Thought the I.R.S. was closing in on him. Crazy as a loon."

"Crazy and good. As it turns out, he's living in East Germany these days. Up north in Rostock."

"I'll be damned. Not a bad choice if you're worried about the I.R.S. Otherwise, I hear they can be a little rough on American spies."

"I hear the same thing. He sent an encrypted cable using dated code to Langley. I don't know how he's living over there, but I've got to hand it to him."

"I can't say I'm surprised. He's definitely a survivor. What did the cable say?"

"More experiments. Just like Voi, only this time in Leipzig. Says he may have a line on similar activity in Warsaw and Prague."

"Sounds like they're opening up an entire front."

"I agree. If there's a lab in Eastern Europe, then it's completely off our radar. If the only one is down your way, then we have a shot at this thing. But if there are three or four more, we're up a serious creek."

"What's Bill think?"

"His gut tells him it's all from one source."

"Any chance of pulling Thompson in?"

"None. We don't even know how to initiate contact with him at this point. Bill's got Arnie Miller working it."

"Arnie'll sniff it out, but we've got to be careful. If the Sovs know we're onto them they'll shift assets, reloc production facilities, or even go operational."

"As usual, no margin for error."

"SOP."

"Keep your head down. Your team absolutely can't be detected. The way I see it, we can't move until we're either sure we have all the labs or the Sovs force our hand."

"I agree. Anything else on your end?"

"That's it. Back to work. Out here."

Nick hangs up. He's spent most of his adult life moving in and out of the shadows. Avoiding detection has been a matter of survival, but this time around the odds are stacked against him. The simple fact of the matter is that there just aren't that many people on St. Thomas. Of the less than 20,000 people living on the island in August of 1962, one tried to kill him less than a month ago, and another spent several hours torturing him four years ago. Neither is likely to forget the face of a man who is the poster child for everything they despise. In spite of his reassurances to the Director, Nick knows that anonymity is already most likely out of reach.

CHAPTER 34

CELL REPLICATION

The message is vague but direct enough to tell him that he'll finally be going into action. His quiet life as the manager of a hardware store in Moline, Illinois will soon come to an end. His chest swells with pride as he once again decodes the message delivered as a simple piece of junk mail soliciting subscriptions to a new 20-volume history of the Second World War.

The lack of contact for more than five years made him wonder if the program had been abandoned. For five years he got up and went to work every day wondering when he'd be called to serve, wondering what the risks would be, wondering if he'd be exposed. He'd survived the worst of the McCarthy era by cutting himself off from all contact with anyone who shared his views. When Sputnik circled the globe he celebrated in private, certain that any day the call would come, a mission would materialize, and his shot at glory, his chance to strike a blow in the American heartland would find its way to his doorstep. Five long years of waiting are about to pay off.

His instructions are to gather, analyze, and summarize the weather patterns in Moline for the month of October for the last ten years. He is also to provide as much detailed information about fluctuations in population clusters by day of the week and time of day for the modest downtown area. Finally, he has been instructed to prepare a personal evacuation plan that will take him as quickly and discreetly as possible to Biloxi, Mississippi, on the Gulf of Mexico.

He decodes the message again. He does so unaware that a high school principal in Fresno, California is doing the same, as is a hairdresser in Chicago, Illinois, and a waiter in St. Louis, Missouri, an auto mechanic in Portland, Maine, and an accountant in Atlanta, Georgia. Each city is now a target, destined to suffer a fate designed as much by cruel ambition as systematic paranoia. Each city's fate will be decided by a global struggle which, in a strange paradox, will go unnoticed by all but a handful of dedicated men and women on both sides of the Iron Curtain.

CHAPTER 35

OLD DOG, OLD TRICKS

After selecting a mango he hopes is ripe, Kyle Richardson pays the sidewalk vendor and heads for the steps of a fountain in the middle of Church Square off of Kronprindsens Gade. The square is three blocks up from the waterfront in Charlotte Amalie, and although by the summer of 1962 it is surrounded by more bars and whorehouses than churches, the name Church Square remains out of local habit.

He sits down on the top step of the fountain, pulls out a pocket knife and begins to peel the mango. It's a beauty. The juice makes a mess of his hands and chin, but he is oblivious. The exotic fruit is practically intoxicating. He knows Carolyn would love it, and he vows to bring her to the islands the next time they get a vacation.

He looks up to see if the few passersby are paying any attention. The men and women in the small noontime crowd, a casual mix of islanders and tourists, go about their business as if Richardson is invisible. Perfect.

As he takes another bite of mango, a figure–a white man, who stands nearly a head taller than all the others–catches his eye. He looks up. Kropotkin! The Russian's severe face is partially hidden by a Panama hat, but Richardson is certain he is looking at one of the Soviet Union's coldest killers. Richardson focuses on him just in time to see him duck into an arched doorway leading to a flight of stairs. Kropotkin takes the stairs two at a time and disappears up the dark, narrow stairway.

Richardson notes the time, calmly finishes his mango, tosses the pit in a nearby garbage can, and wipes his hands on his handkerchief. When he is done, he stops the first islander to cross his path.

"Do you mind if I ask you something?"

"Go ahead, man."

Richardson points to the two-story stucco building Kropotkin just entered.

"What's on the second floor?"

"Calypso Willy's. They got drinks and ladies. Which one you want? Both maybe?"

"No. Just wondering. Thanks."

"Okay, but I know a better place near Red Hook on the east end if you change your mind. Know what I mean?"

"I'll pass. Thanks anyway."

Richardson heads south from the square for the waterfront. He's scheduled to meet the owner of a 36-foot Chris-Craft Constellation available for charter. He decides he'll return to the square circling around from the north after his meeting and after a quick call to Nick. Maybe he'll get lucky and spot Kropotkin on his way out of the bar. He won't stay long. No sense pushing it. If Kropotkin sees him, he may pick a different bar the next time the spirit moves him. Worse yet, he may recognize him from their shootout in Berlin and report back to Moscow that the Americans are in town. But if Kropotkin settles into a pattern as a repeat customer then he's as stupid as he is dangerous. In that case, Nick and his team will have him by the balls.

CHAPTER 36

GATHERING FORCES

"Dmitri! Wait for me."

Dmitri stops until his friend catches up.

"Give me a cigarette."

Dimitri hands his friend a cigarette. They smoke as they walk.

"Where are you going?"

"To the gulag."

"Don't joke. Besides, there isn't any more gulag."

"Okay, then, Yuri. You tell me why the KGB wants to talk to me."

"I don't know why anyone would want to talk to you. I used to enjoy my life. Then I made the mistake one day of talking to you."

"I see. Then it is you who has denounced me. That is why the KGB is so interested in me all of a sudden."

"Fool. They're talking to everyone in the regiment."

"Then we're all going to the gulag."

"Maybe the rest of us, but the KGB would never send you."

"I'm not even good enough for the gulag?"

"They're afraid you'd destroy morale!"

"Now that's something I'll drink to."

"A huge surprise, my friend."

With that the two life-long friends–both of them mechanics serving in the second regiment of the 43rd Guards Rocket Division of the 43rd Red Banner Rocket Army of the Soviet Strategic Rocket Forces–share a laugh on their way back to the motor pool to finish another round of scheduled maintenance on the regiment's trailers for its R-12, nuclear-tipped ballistic missiles.

The 43rd Guards Rocket Division, headquartered outside of the northern Ukrainian town of Romny, finds itself host to more than the usual contingent of KGB officers these days. The division's brass has instructed the regimental commanders to make their missile crews available for interviews by the KGB to determine each crew's suitability for an important training mission. What that mission is, no one can say, because as of the summer of 1962, no one at division level or below knows.

What the division's three regimental commanders do know is that the mission involves transporting their men and equipment via rail to the Black Sea port of Sevastopol near the southern end of the Crimean Peninsula. They also know that once they are in Sevastopol special units of stevedores temporarily attached to the division will load the regiments' equipment onto civilian freighters commandeered specifically for their mission. And they know that once all men and materiel are at sea, they will finally be given detailed orders about their mission. Until then, it will be their job as commanders to manage the men's discipline and morale in the face of constantly shifting rumors and speculation. Fortunately, the amount of work required to prepare for the unprecedented move is nothing short of extraordinary, leaving Dmitri Bogdonevitch, Yuri Belyavski and the more than 500 men of their missile regiment, men who think nothing of working around the most sophisticated and destructive weapons their country has produced, little time for idle chatter.

CHAPTER 37

THE EAST CHECKS IN

Arnie Miller, the CIA's Berlin Station Chief, waits next to a payphone near the entrance to the Oskar-Helene-Heim U-Bahn station in West Berlin. The message from Cliff Thompson came first thing this morning: be at the phone booth at 5:00 p.m. Miller knows Thompson's reputation as a maverick, but he also knows Thompson isn't inclined to waste his or anyone else's time. So he waits.

Thompson's disappearance more than a year ago, or more accurately his lack of contact with the station for more than a year, is one of the mysteries Miller hopes to clear up if he can set up a meeting. When Miller learned from Langley that Thompson was operating in the Rostock area, he sent a courier on a launch out of Copenhagen to rendezvous with a Polish diesel mechanic who was turned after his entire family was shipped off to prison for being in the wrong place at the wrong time during the Poznan riots in 1956. The mechanic, who works on the waterfront in Rostock, confirmed he's been hearing bits and pieces about an American agent working the area for the last six months. The courier passed on Miller's instructions to do whatever was necessary to make contact with Thompson.

The mechanic, at best a gifted amateur, took a shot at a lengthy and dangerous run through Rostock's waterfront bars and cafés. When Thompson got word from a robust, accommodating barmaid that the Pole was looking for him he started a search of his own. Finding and then cornering the mechanic in an alleyway was too easy for a pro like

Thompson. The mechanic was two seconds from getting his throat slit when he convinced Thompson of his connection to Arnie Miller. Thompson spared the man's life. He then relayed a message to the Berlin Station Chief via Gdansk using the comms room of a Lithuanian freighter whose captain lives for the privilege of shoving it to the Russian occupiers of his homeland.

The payphone rings. Miller slides in and picks up the receiver.

"I got it."

"Fifteen minutes."

"Where?"

"How 'bout some home cooking?"

"I'll be there."

Miller hangs up and heads to his Zehlendorf office surmising, correctly, that Thompson's oblique reference to home cooking refers to the modest turn-of-the-century house that has served as the CIA's unassuming headquarters in Berlin for nearly 15 years.

"Send him in, Laura."

Moments later the door to Arnie Miller's first floor office opens and Cliff Thompson walks in.

"Jesus Christ, Thompson. Give me one good reason I shouldn't have you arrested on the spot."

"How about because you don't have anyone working for you who can slip back and forth across the Iron Curtain as easily as I can?"

"You know, we've given that some thought, and it doesn't take a genius to figure you're working both sides of the curtain."

"That's a chance you're going to have to take."

"What've you got?"

"Whatever these guys are cooking, my bet is they're cooking it all in one spot."

"Leipzig?"

"Negative. Same thing for Prague and Warsaw. Experiments were conducted after receipts of shipments from across the pond. That's all I've got, but it's solid."

"Nothing more definite? A country? A continent?"

"Gotta leave something for you guys to do."

"Yeah, thanks. How are you living?"

"I had some cash when I jumped, most of it from you guys, and STASI pays me in west marks to feed them bullshit."

"How long can that last?"

"Tough to say. Trips like this boost my credibility. They'll debrief me tomorrow or the next day, and I'll tell them something they want to hear."

"Why not stay over here?"

"Where's the fun in that?"

"Where's the fun in getting a bullet in your brain, or haven't you heard about those guys?"

"Your concern is touching. Time to go."

Thompson stands to leave.

"How do I get in touch with you?"

"You don't. I'll check in if I've got something for you."

"You need anything? Cash?"

"I'm okay for now. I'll let you know."

Thompson heads for the door.

"Cliff."

He stops and turns around.

"It's good to see you. I thought for sure you were a corpse."

Thompson smiles, turns, and leaves the office.

Arnie Miller picks up his phone.

"Laura. Get me the secure line to Langley. I need to talk to Bill Johnson."

CHAPTER 38

AN ODD COUPLE

Schnelling sits at his kitchen table trying to review the specs of a variety of small, portable, pressurized containers. His nerves are already frayed when he hears the front door to his small bungalow open and then slam shut. He glances at his watch – precisely 1:30 p.m. Kropotkin, as has been the case every other day for the last ten days, left Schnelling alone at 11:00 this morning. His punctual return at 1:30 each day is a blessing and a curse. Schnelling resolves to head for his lab the next time Kropotkin goes wandering. However, he realizes that any pattern of activity by Kropotkin, if discovered, can render them both vulnerable.

Kropotkin belches as he plops himself down on the living room's small couch. Schnelling, concerned about how his oafish roommate's lack of discretion could jeopardize his mission, summons up enough courage to ask the beast some pointed questions. He folds the pages of specs under his arm and heads into the living room.

"Where the devil do you go when you leave here?"

Kropotkin lights a cigarette and ignores the question.

"You know I could set my watch by your coming and going. And if I can, that means anyone watching us can, too. You might as well take out an ad in the paper if you're . . ."

"Prostitutes," Kropotkin blurts out.

"What?"

"You heard me, old man. Prostitutes. And keep your fucking nose out of my business."

"You fool!"

"Only fool, old fool like you, would sit around in this stinking climate and not want woman. Or do you prefer little boys, Nazi filth?"

Kropotkin laughs at his own crude joke before he continues to smoke.

As Schnelling tries to maintain his dignity, he makes the mistake of responding.

"I prefer the company of men and women of refinement, but I am stuck with you."

"Okay, Professor Asshole. You have one more week. If you don't take me to lab I will pull its location out of you surgically."

Schnelling, mortified by the turn his life has taken, flees the bungalow with Kropotkin's malevolent laugh ringing in his ears.

Nick Temple sits in a Jeep Utility Wagon twenty meters down the street from Schnelling's house. Nick followed Kropotkin at a safe distance after the Russian left his new favorite hangout on Church Square. The hunch paid off. Nick instantly recognizes Schnelling as one of the two men he heard speaking German at Sleepy Pete's. Nick focuses his Nikon F single lens reflex camera. Bull's-eye!

CHAPTER 39

BAITING THE TRAP

Nick Temple, Kyle Richardson, Dalila Atieno and Pete Hall finish breakfast on the veranda of the small, mountainside house that has been serving as the team's headquarters. Nick rented the unassuming three-bedroom home from a former Aramco executive on a tip from Hugh Ridgely. When it became clear the team would be staying on the island for more than a week, they checked out of the Virgin Isle Hotel to set up shop for the foreseeable future in their current digs.

The house sits alone on more than an acre at the end of a quarter-mile driveway leading up from the main house occupied by Ridgely's former colleague. It's the last place in the world anyone would suspect of being occupied by a team of CIA agents tasked with thwarting a vile and deadly plot by the Soviet Union.

The delivery to the house of two steamer trunks from Miami via San Juan courtesy of Leeward Shipping went without a hitch and, more importantly, without prompting any questions at the transfer point. The trunks contain the team's modest array of communications and intercept equipment, weapons, ammunition, flares, and explosives requisitioned by Bill Johnson before Nick left Langley.

"That's it then. We know where the professor is, and we know that Kropotkin can't keep it in his pants. Odd days of the week. He'll be back day after tomorrow. No doubt about it."

Kyle Richardson nods his head in agreement.

"The timing's like clockwork. You sure this guy isn't German?"

"Russian through and through. I can tell you from experience, and I have the scars to prove it. Dalila, how do you feel about posing as a prostitute?"

"Posing only, right?"

"You're the receptionist, front desk, face of the organization, nothing more. It's about timing," Nick tries to assure her.

"He's not going down without a fight," Richardson points out.

"You're right. We're going to need some firepower," Nick agrees.

"If it's us, the word will spread and our cover, if we still have any, will be blown."

"I'm open to suggestions."

Pete Hall, who can barely believe that he's listening to CIA agents putting together a small operation, speaks up.

"What about Puerto Rico? Don't you guys have any assets there?"

Nick immediately recognizes the suggestion for what it is.

"Great idea. We don't, but the Army does. The Puerto Rican National Guard's 65th Infantry Regiment to be exact. There should be an MP unit attached to it. Kyle, get Langley on it. We need two men here tonight. Nothing special. Just a couple of good, tough cops."

Kyle Richardson gulps down his coffee and stands up.

"I'll head down to Government House. Anything else for the folks back home?"

"Tell them to alert the local constable. We'll need his cooperation to get Dalila in there without any fuss."

Nick reaches into his shirt pocket and pulls out a roll of 35mm film in a small tin container and tosses it to Richardson.

"Have that put in the D.C. pouch for Bill Johnson. We'll see if we can't find out who our professor is."

"Got it."

Richardson heads back through the house to the gravel parking lot in front, climbs into the team's rented Jeep Utility Wagon, and heads down the mountain for Charlotte Amalie.

Back on the veranda, Nick and Dalila go over her limited role in the sting.

"There's a phone at the desk, and there are a couple of chairs in the waiting area."

"I can call after he's gone to a room."

"We'll start there, but we need a backup. I don't trust the phone system. Maybe we can wire a room for sound."

Nick turns to Pete Hall.

"Pete, ever been in a Caribbean whorehouse?"

"Nope. Sorry to say I've never been in any kind of whorehouse."

"How'd you like to take a shot at some undercover work?"

"I'm in."

"If we can't get the room wired, we'll put you in the waiting room before Kropotkin's arrival. When he gets taken to one of the rooms in the back, you head downstairs. We'll have our cops from Puerto Rico out by the fountain or the market. You just come out of that doorway and head for the waterfront. That'll be the signal that Kropotkin's, shall we say, engaged."

"I doubt an engagement is what he's after," Dalila suggests.

"Just trying to keep it clean."

"You mean like that crack about not keeping it in his pants?" Dalila asks.

Nick winces. He's been making a special effort to mind his language when he's around Dalila, but old habits die hard.

"Nobody's perfect."

"Don't worry about me. You keep worrying about my feelings and you're going to make a mistake."

"No shit."

"That's better," Dalila quips.

"If we can get a bug in the room, then we'll hold you in reserve until Dalila gets out of there."

Nick looks at his watch.

"We need to pick up our charter. Maybe we can spot this lab from the water."

"You think the professor will make a move once Kropotkin's out of the way?" Pete asks.

"That's our best judgment. Now that we know where he lives, I want to be ready for him if he heads back to work."

The three of them, Nick, Dalila, and Pete, enjoy a quiet moment engaged in their separate thoughts about what lies ahead. Pete Hall, who should be grading the lab work of graduate students, works hard to contain his excitement at the thought of going into action with the CIA. Dalila Atieno, who should be working on the myriad details of the complex task of transitioning a former colony to a fully independent and sovereign nation, reflects on the seamy details of work in the trenches of the world's most dangerous geopolitical game. And Nick Temple, who is precisely where he should be, marvels at the selfless courage of his two newest colleagues.

CHAPTER 40

SECOND THOUGHTS

"Over here. We'll sit."

Zenaida motions to a bench along the river across from the Kremlin. Yevgeny helps Tatyana, his three-year old daughter, up onto the bench. She sits between her parents without fidgeting. Yevgeny looks around to make sure no one is within earshot.

"There's nothing to be done about it now, is there?" Zenaida asks.

"No, but the diversion is taking over. The military is so enamored of the plan that they are talking as if a nuclear strike is desirable, a nuclear war with the Americans is winnable."

"They've lost their minds."

"The process has taken on an inertia of its own. I rarely hear of anything else. The original strike is an afterthought. The diversion we created for the Americans is diverting us."

"Where do you go with this?"

"Nowhere. I do my work, and that is all I can do. But we're losing control of the situation on the American island. I spend all of my time answering idiotic questions about a plan that is not really a plan."

"And where is the General Secretary?"

"Disappeared. I think he spends all of his time with generals and colonels."

"Then leave it to him. It's simple. It's out of your hands."

"And when both plans fail, it is my head, not my hands that will pay the price."

"Don't talk like that. Not in front of your daughter. Not in front of me either," Zenaida scolds him.

Yevgeny stares across the river at the Kremlin, the cradle of power in the Soviet Union. Too many men–important men who occupied the highest positions of power, heroic men who fought the tsarists and the counterrevolutionaries, who fought the fascists, who marched in the streets, and who marched to Berlin–have been dragged from their offices in the Kremlin to the basement of the Lubyanka on their way to Siberia or worse. His fear for his own fate is tempered by his almost genetic Russian fatalism.

"I will work, you will raise Tatyana, and life will bring what it brings."

"In the meantime?"

"In the meantime, I will do as I'm told by my most important boss, my beautiful wife!"

"Or she and your beautiful daughter will run into the arms of the first American who will give us a villa with servants and a cherry orchard in exchange for the most important secrets of their dreaded enemy."

"You know such an American?"

"I was hoping you would introduce us. You're the one with the connections."

They both laugh lightly.

"How about a dacha on the Crimean?"

"With a cherry orchard?"

"Exactly as you wish."

Zenaida stands.

"We should be going. Our apartment will have to do for the time being."

Yevgeny gathers Tatyana in his arms. The small Kasparanov family turns back down the path that led them to this point, back to the small, bugged apartment they have the audacity to call their own.

CHAPTER 41

THE WRONG SIDE OF THE LIMB

Hartmut Schnelling can't stop sweating. He removes his wire-frame glasses and wipes them clean with his handkerchief. He folds his handkerchief neatly and returns it to his pants pocket. He puts his glasses back on before he resumes pacing in his small living room. Another day with no word from Moscow. He is certain he followed protocol in his last transmission. He is just as certain that a response should have come yesterday via wire. The fact that another 24 hours has passed and he has still heard nothing is a cause of deep concern for the professor. In all of his dealings with Kasparanov he has never experienced a lapse in communications. The notion of communication inflexibility was drilled into his head during his indoctrination. He can still hear the political officer's stern admonition repeated over and over again: "Never deviate from the established transmission matrix. Never!"

Has the mission been scrubbed? Has operational responsibility been transferred? Are his sponsors in Moscow headed for prison? Or, God forbid, is Kropotkin his only link? He can't make any sense of the turn of events. The formula works, as the tests so brutally demonstrate; effective dispersal is ridiculously and brilliantly simple; formula production targets are on pace to be exceeded; all cells are on alert; and existing funds have been disbursed. Everything required for a successful, silent, and devastating strike against the United States is either in place or ahead of schedule.

And where is Kropotkin? The specter of Kropotkin, even when he isn't brooding about Schnelling's house, grinds away at Schnelling's personal sense of security.

What was sure to be a triumphant strike against the Americans a few weeks ago is spiraling out of control. He curses himself for not anticipating Russian ineptitude, for fooling himself into believing that somehow the Russians had magically transformed themselves into dedicated, disciplined technicians capable of adhering to a detailed, specific plan. He knew that asking them to do anything beyond sacrificing tens of thousands of men in hopeless battle after hopeless battle would be a gamble, but he convinced himself that by retaining control of key aspects of the operation he would be able to make up for what he considers predictable Russian bungling. And now it appears he was wrong, that the entire operation is falling apart on the threshold of its implementation. In the mind of Professor Hartmut Schnelling, the only way for the operation to be salvaged is for it to be turned over to him personally in its entirety. That means, to begin with, the elimination of Kropotkin.

CHAPTER 42

GET IN LINE

The two friends see the line forming and join the others. A middle-aged woman in front of them turns. She can't help noticing one man's crutches and missing right leg. She gestures for the two veterans to go ahead of her in line.

"Please," she says.

"We are fine here. Thank you for your kindness," the man on crutches responds. He lights a cigarette.

Like all Muscovites, the men are accustomed to standing in lines; like nearly all Muscovites, they will gladly stand in line for ice cream.

"I think we'll have an early winter this year. More cold weather, even more than we're used to," the smoking man's companion muses.

"The weather is a funny thing. What we feel here is affected by weather in parts of the world that are rarely noticed," the veteran on crutches replies.

More Muscovites gather behind the two men as the line moves slowly towards the ice cream vendor at the Moscow River embankment.

A man wearing a gray suit, a royal blue shirt, and a black fedora approaches the veterans. His shirt's color is identical to the background color of KGB shoulder boards. He sometimes wears it as a courtesy to his fellow citizens, his way of letting them know they are to take extra care in his presence. He stops. The woman in front of the veterans leaves the line in a hurry at the sight of the man in the royal blue shirt.

"What are they selling here?" he asks the veteran on crutches.

The veteran takes another drag on his cigarette before responding.

"I don't know. I just saw the line and got in it."

They both laugh at the old Russian joke born out of a need to see humor in deprivation.

"I'll take her place," the man in the fedora says as he slips into the line in front of the veterans. He knows no one in the line will dare object.

The smoking veteran throws his cigarette on the ground. The KGB agent puts it out with his foot.

"You shouldn't smoke. It's bad for your health."

"Many things are bad for my health."

"It would be nice to take a vacation in the tropics."

"What do you recommend?"

"The Black Sea over the Caribbean."

"What if I've already bought my ticket?"

"See if you can get a refund. Anyone holding such a ticket is a target."

"Is that your personal opinion?"

"It is, but I don't agree with it."

They both chuckle at the standard quip from the worst days of the Stalinist era. The one-legged veteran lights another cigarette. The line continues to inch forward.

"Your young travelling companion may be forced to change his plans."

With that, the man in the fedora leaves as abruptly as he came. The veterans gaze after him.

"He works for Proykiev."

"He's taking an awful risk."

"Maybe he wants Proykiev to fail."

"He will. He should never have sent that fool Kropotkin. He'll make a dog's breakfast of it."

"Will you tell our young friend?"

"He'll have to figure it out on his own."

"A man goes on a journey?"

"Quoting Tolstoy? Are you now a member of the intelligentsia?"

"Never. It's too dangerous. I'd rather be back in Berlin killing fascists."

They chuckle once more. The line moves again, slowly inching its way towards a small, sweet diversion from the mundane brutality that is too often life in the Soviet Union's capital city.

CHAPTER 43

THE VIEW FROM THE WATER

Nick sits at the portside helm of the 36-foot Chris-Craft Constellation and slowly guides the boat through the clear waters of the Atlantic off the north coast of St. Thomas. Dalila sits next to him scanning the coastline for any sign of a laboratory through Nick's Bausch & Lomb Zephyr 7x35 binoculars. Kyle Richardson and Pete Hall make half-hearted attempts at fishing off the boat's stern from time to time for the sake of cover.

A detailed chart of the coast and the immediate offshore waters sits in front of the boat's wheel. Nick scans the chart constantly, mindful of the area's dangerous reefs and sandbars. A slight breeze from due north works on the boat's modest freeboard and forces Nick to make constant, subtle adjustment's to maintain course. Offshore and away from the surf, the boat glides easily, steadily, making Dalila's job manageable.

Since negotiating the channel between St. Thomas and Thatch Cay they've surveyed the coastline of every bay and inlet: a quick inspection of diminutive Tutu Bay just northwest of the channel; a more extended scan of the popular and expansive Magens Bay; a return trip for Nick to Hull Bay, the site of his clumsy surfing attempts; then into another channel, this one between Neltjeberg Bay to port and Inner Brass Island to starboard. Dalila scours the coast as they motor slowly through the channel before continuing on past two more small bays – Mail and then Caret to the west. A finger of rocks protrudes into the Atlantic west of Caret Bay, after which Nick heads south to stay parallel to the coastline. As they passed the point of land separating Hendrik and Santa Maria Bays, Nick throttles both engines back to a speed that barely allows him to maintain headway and steerage.

"Kyle, take the wheel."

Richardson reels in his line, secures his hook to an eye on his rod, stows the rod and heads for the wheelhouse.

"We're coming up on Santa Maria Bay. The maps show the ruins of an old sugar plantation at the northeast end of the bay. Sounds like a perfect place to hide a lab. I want to take a good look."

Nick grabs a second pair of binoculars out of his sea bag stowed in the forward cabin as Kyle takes the wheel. He returns to the wheelhouse and positions himself next to Dalila. It doesn't take long before he spots the ruins.

"There. Just below the bluff separating it from Hendrik Bay."

Nick points to what he and Dalila see simultaneously: the remains of a sugar plantation's round, stone mill tower rising out of a dense tangle of growth. The southern side of the tower is being overtaken by thick climbing vines. Another two or three years and the stonework will be completely covered and hidden from view.

They scan the surrounding terrain carefully, looking for buildings, man-made clearings, signs of jeep trails or roads, antennae, anything to indicate the ruins are in current use.

"Anything?" Nick asks Dalila.

"Only the tower," she responds without lowering her binoculars.

"Kyle, take us back around. I want to take one more look. Take us east of the point and then we'll come back around for another look."

"Got it."

Richardson opens the throttles slightly to increase his control during the turn. He cuts the wheel to starboard. In short order they are at the turnaround point, ready for a second pass.

Behind the dense growth on St. Thomas's north shore, in one of the small buildings above Santa Maria Bay which houses the successful experiments of Hartmut Schnelling, at one of the few windows in the complex, the professor sits watching as Nick's chartered Chris-Craft motors slowly east again before heading west just beyond the point. His third look at the craft and its occupants convinces him.

"The American is back," he says to himself. "This time with reinforcements."

Schnelling drops his binoculars as he frets about the additional American manpower. Then it hits him. A mission for Kropotkin! If he can convince Kropotkin of the need to eliminate the Americans, then he'll achieve two goals at once: the elimination of the increasing threat from the U.S., and a change in focus for the malevolent Kropotkin. And should Kropotkin fail, the Soviets might recall him or even terminate him, a sublime proposition as far as the professor is concerned. But none of it can happen until he can reestablish contact with Moscow. Why has he heard nothing? Where is Kasparanov? How much further can or should he proceed with production without instructions from the Kremlin?

Schnelling once again trains his binoculars on the waters of Santa Maria Bay just in time to see the Americans motor west out of sight. He checks his watch. Kropotkin's thrice weekly "visit" will end soon. He'll have to continue his work on the final production logistics the day after tomorrow. For now it is enough to know that with luck Kropotkin will be otherwise engaged for the immediate future.

CHAPTER 44

SAN JUAN MUSCLE

Nick eases the Constellation alongside the finger pier on the waterfront east of Frenchtown. Two men wait on the dock. Both men are in their early thirties. They wear panama hats, gray, short-sleeve, square-bottom shirts, dark slacks and loafers. Their Ray Ban aviator sunglasses complete the uniform.

"Toss your bow line," the taller of the two men directs Kyle Richardson. Kyle complies.

The man secures the line to a cleat on the pier. Nick shifts into reverse and by opening the throttles slightly brings the boat to a complete stop. Dalila jumps onto the dock with the stern line and secures it.

Nick cuts the engines and inspects the lines to make sure they're taut. A representative from the charter company, clipboard and pen in hand, walks down the dock to where the Chris-Craft is tied up. He inspects the exterior of the boat quickly, climbs on board, and does another cursory inspection of the boat's interior, including its forward cabin.

"Everything seems to be in order. Just make sure all of your gear is off loaded."

He makes a series of check marks on the form on his clipboard before offering the clipboard and pen to Kyle Richardson.

"If you'll just sign right there at the bottom, Mr. Mahan."

Richardson signs the form. The representative tears out a carbon copy and hands it to him.

"Keys?"

"Right here."

Nick tosses the keys to the man who catches them and puts them in his pocket.

"That'll do it, then. Been a pleasure doing business with you. Call whenever you need a boat. I'm your man."

Kyle thanks him and shakes his hand. They watch as the man leaves the dock, gets into his car, and drives away.

"Mr. Mahan?" Nick asks.

"Johnson's favorite alias. It's on about half of his counterfeit passports. I stole it since he's not in the field anymore."

"Kind of like an inheritance?"

"Yeah, kind of. Who are these guys?" Kyle points to the two men who helped them tie up the boat. One of them steps forward.

"Lieutenant Raoul Escobar, and this is Staff Sergeant Cristobal Guzman. We're from the 65th in San Juan. I understand you need some help."

Nick shakes both of their hands.

"Nice to meet you. Indeed we do. Let's get you introduced. I'm Nick Temple and I suppose I'm in charge of this small outfit. This is Dalila Atieno. We stole her from the Brits in Nairobi. Their loss, our gain. That's Pete Hall. Pete's a professor at Johns Hopkins on loan to us for the duration. And this young man is Kyle Richardson, ex-marine, soon-to-be-father, and probably a CIA lifer."

They all exchange handshakes as the two newest members of team Temple are brought into the fold.

"Your car in the lot?" Nick asks the Lieutenant.

"It's a rental we picked up in town after landing."

"Gear?"

"In the car."

"Perfect. Let's get to it."

With Nick in the lead, the five men and one woman walk down the finger pier heading for the small parking lot just onshore.

Nick engages Lieutenant Escobar in some chit chat as they make their way to the team's cars.

"Come here by seaplane?"

"That was the first thing available."

"What's *your* availability?"

"As long as you need. That's straight from D.C."

"What we have in mind shouldn't take more than a couple of days, but you're welcome to stick around after that. There's going to be more work to do. We need to get you men up to speed. We'll put you up for the next couple of nights. The accommodations aren't luxurious, but they're secure. Hope you don't mind sleeping on the floor."

"We'll take whatever you've got," Lieutenant Escobar responds.

"All right, then. Let's get going. You can follow me to your new quarters. We're in the wagon."

"Lead the way."

CHAPTER 45

SAME OLD, SAME OLD

Bill Johnson and the Director have been down this road before: the Berlin Blockade in '48 and '49; the Hydrogen Bomb in '53; Suez, Budapest, and Poznan in '56; Sputnik in '57; Powers, Gagarin and Berlin again in '61. Since the end of World War II the rhythm of their professional lives has been defined by events originating behind the Iron Curtain. Their perceptions and judgments of a society largely closed to outsiders are fine tuned to a degree the average American cannot understand. Where others see threats directed at the free world, they discern pleas for political survival directed at a scheming inner circle; where the unskilled believe they've spotted a weakness, they sense a trap; where demagogues see totalitarian bloodlust, they detect old wine in new jugs – an ageless xenophobia. And where others see little or nothing at all, they see the potential for trouble on a massive scale. Today, Bill Johnson and the Director see nothing but trouble.

"I don't think any other conclusion is reasonable. It's definitely all tied together, sir. The railhead activity and the uptick in merchant marine deployment from both Vladivostok and Sevastopol. It's all connected."

"No chance of a bumper crop, that it's just harvest time and these deployments have a civilian application?"

"Too early, and the locations are inconsistent with that analysis, sir."

"Yeah, I know. I was only half serious."

"Any port in a storm, right?" Johnson lets his boss off the hook.

"What's the Army hearing in Sinop?"

"Soviet military units are supplanting stevedores and other dockworkers in Sevastopol. Whatever they're loading is 'eyes only' and the civilians are getting kicked to the curb. That's what got the attention of one of our assets in the Crimean. Sinop confirmed it."

"We should be able to pick up the maritime traffic in Istanbul."

"Sure. We'll be ready when they come through, but at that point, unless they get sloppy, it's just about counting ships. We'll still have no idea where they're headed, although we might have a lead on what they're carrying. And so far, whatever else this operation has been, it sure as hell hasn't been sloppy."

"What about Berlin?"

"Besides the Field Station?"

"Right. Arnie Miller. Anything coming his way?"

"Not a thing. Arnie's been working Cliff Thompson behind the curtain on the St. Thomas operation. That's still producing some solid intel, but nothing in his zone appears related to these new developments."

"Vladivostok?"

"Buttoned up. Nothing solid, but our man is reporting some of the same sort of activity we're seeing in Sevastopol. So far the Sovs have managed to keep a tight lid on what's next."

"What about the railheads?"

"Most are routine. Of the routes we've been able to confirm, and it's not a whole lot of them, the railhead that jumps out could hold the key to the entire operation."

"Well?"

"Romny. In the Ukraine."

"Why is that name familiar?"

"It's a stone's throw from the 43rd Guards Rocket Division H.Q."

"Jesus H. Christ!"

The Director leans back in his chair absorbing the details of his conversation with Johnson, putting it all in the context of his experience. After a quiet moment he slowly leans forward, placing his elbows on his desk, his eyes wide open, almost in alarm.

"Do you see it, Bill?"

"I'll tell you what I see: a redeployment of significant assets of the Soviet Union's nuclear forces."

"No doubt about it."

"With no idea as to where or why."

"We figure out where, and that'll tell us why."

"Agreed."

"What the hell is Ivan up to now?" the Director muses aloud.

Answering that simple question has been the raison d'être for these two men since the spring of 1945.

CHAPTER 46

CHECKING THE MAIL

Nick pulls the Jeep Utility Wagon up to the team's mountainside headquarters and billets. Raoul Escobar and Cristobal Guzman park their 1962 Rambler 400 convertible to the Jeep's right. Kyle, Pete and Dalila head inside. Nick holds back to have a word with the team's newest recruits.

"Grab your equipment, Lieutenant. We'll do an inventory, and pull what we need for the op."

The Lieutenant nods to Sergeant Guzman who heads for the Rambler's trunk.

"How about if we skip the rank and stick to names?" Escobar suggests.

"Agreed. You and Cristobal join the others. Kyle will brief you. I've got to head for Government House."

Guzman pulls a canvas sea bag out of the Rambler's trunk. He and Escobar walk up the small sidewalk, onto the house's front porch, swing open the screen door and go inside.

Nick climbs into the Jeep. Just as he is about to start the engine, Dalila, still sporting the light blue scarf she wore on their working cruise, comes out of the house.

"Wait. I'm going with you."

She opens the passenger door of the Jeep and steps in.

"I take it I'm cleared for Government House," she says as she flashes Nick her usual brilliant smile.

Nick starts the Jeep and throws it into reverse.

"Indeed you are."

Nick executes a K-turn in the narrow driveway and heads down the hill.

"We're just picking up a packet from Langley."

"What are you expecting?"

"Any information on the professor's identity from the roll of film I shot."

"Can we do a bit of shopping after?"

"What are we looking for?"

"I'm afraid my wardrobe doesn't have anything suitable for the receptionist at a house of prostitution."

"I'm not surprised. Sure, but I'll be honest; I don't know where the shops for that sort of outfit are."

"I do. I've been keeping my eyes open."

They reach the bottom of the drive. Nick turns left onto Brewers Bay Road heading east for Charlotte Amalie.

"Will it be dangerous?"

"It could be for Escobar and Guzman. It shouldn't be for you. Kropotkin is a machine. Taking him down is going to take timing, skill, and instantly overwhelming force."

"How will you manage the timing?"

"We're going to wire the room for sound. I'll wear a receiver. When the audio indicates Kropotkin is focused on the hooker, that's when I'll send them in to grab him."

Dalila can't help smirking.

"Men using their weaknesses against each other. It's rather amusing, don't you think?"

"Hysterical, actually. I wish I could be there when Kropotkin gets caught quite literally with his pants down."

"What if it goes badly?"

"If you hear any shooting at all, get the hell out of there. Don't hesitate. Shots will mean Kropotkin's put up a fight. No. That's wrong. Get out as soon as Escobar and Guzman arrive. There's no need for you to wait around. Kyle and I will be on the square for backup. I don't think it'll come to that, but you need to be ready to move if it does. Escobar and Guzman will hand him over to us. Kyle and I will take it from there."

Nick guides the Jeep along the narrow road with dense vegetation on either side giving it the feeling of a tunnel.

"He tortured you?"

"A long time ago. He's a sick bastard, so it'll be a pleasure taking him down."

"Termination?"

"We're not playing checkers, sweetheart. What did you think was going to happen?"

Dalila doesn't respond. Instead, she stares straight ahead, remaining silent for the rest of the drive.

They pass Truman Airport, drive through Frenchtown and on into Charlotte Amalie. Nick navigates his way through the town's narrow streets before he parks on Kongens Gade across from Government House. He turns off the engine and removes the key. Before getting out, he turns to Dalila.

"Second thoughts?"

"None."

"What then?"

Dalila puts her hand on Nick's arm.

"I find myself worrying about your safety more than my own."

"I recall being warned about that."

"I know, but it's not something I can help. Not now."

Nick takes her hand in his.

"Come on. Let's find out who our professor is. Then I'll take you shopping for your hooker dress."

Dalila smiles softly.

"You certainly know how to spoil a girl."

They get out of the Jeep and cross the street towards the front steps of the ornate, three-story, neoclassical structure. As they walk Dalila grabs Nick's arm and Nick puts his hand on hers. The veteran American CIA agent and the unassuming Kenyan bureaucrat–the most unlikely of couples–simultaneously contemplate what few couples ever have to face: the potential impact the apparent shift in their hitherto professional relationship could have not only for themselves, but also for their countries, and even for the world.

Dalila Atieno is silent. She knows she is in no position to argue with the simple calculation of a small group of men west of the Iron Curtain that for the sake of their country and the sake of the world Kropotkin must die.

CHAPTER 47

THE INNER CIRCLE'S SHARP EDGE

Yevgeny Kasparanov has been unable to sleep since a summons to an audience with the Deputy Commissar of the KGB's First Chief Directorate, Alexander Proykiev, was hand-delivered to his office two days ago. Such a summons is usually the beginning of the end for its recipient. This morning, after two sleepless nights, his terror has given way to resignation, to classic Russian fatalism. He knows that when the machine which is Moscow politics gets unleashed and pointed in a particular direction there is no resisting its strength. His only hope was the General Secretary, but Kasparanov's repeated requests over the last 48 hours for an appointment have been ignored as if they had never been made. And now he must simply accept his fate. His only hope is that his wife and daughter will somehow be provided for or at least spared.

He is about to leave his office for his ten o'clock meeting when Proykiev storms in.

"Sit," Proykiev orders as he slams the office door shut behind him. "Sit!"

Kasparanov, stunned by this development, sits at his desk as ordered. Proykiev immediately starts pacing; Kasparanov can see he is agitated.

"I have come here as a courtesy to you. After all, you are, for the time being, the author of a strategic plan that has been embraced by the highest authorities in the Party. Do you understand?"

Proykiev punctuates his inquisition by punching his left palm with his right fist.

Kasparanov, owing to fatigue and the sudden shock of Proykiev's appearance in his office, fails to answer.

"As I thought. I'll be blunt. You are in danger of being condemned as a counterrevolutionary, a self-aggrandizing narcissist, and reactionary defeatist. Your insistence that this ridiculous scheme that hinges on the questionable loyalties of an avowed fascist, an enemy of the people of the Soviet Union, be carried out can only be attributed to your failure to set aside your personal, bourgeois ambitions in favor of the collective good."

Kasparanov manages to stifle the urge to ask Proykiev if he is hallucinating, if Proykiev perhaps thinks he is talking to himself. Instead, gathering his composure, he asks a simple question.

"And what is the source of this danger?"

"You!" Proykiev thunders. "You have brought any misery you and your family may experience on yourself and them."

The severity of Proykiev's attack is not surprising to Kasparanov. What is surprising is the clear agitation of a man renowned for his sang-froid.

"Can such a state of affairs be avoided? For my family? For my daughter?"

Proykiev continues as if he did not hear the question.

"Schnelling is as good as dead. We have his pitiable communiqués to you that are nothing more than a litany of his failures. Kropotkin has his orders, and I am confident I will receive news at any moment of their execution. This fantastic scheme of yours has been deemed a failure and you are never to mention it again. You will be reassigned. You owe this courtesy to the fact that in certain circles the Cuban affair still bears your name. So long as that is the case, you will not be arrested. You will continue to make yourself available. Do you understand?"

"Understood, Comrade Proykiev."

"That is all."

Proykiev executes a swift about face and slams the door to Kasparanov's small office behind him.

Yevgeny Kasparanov, who could practically feel the noose tightening around his neck no more than ten minutes ago, exhales and falls back into his chair. He sits for a moment as he tries to sort out the morning's extraordinary turn of events.

To begin with, rather than coming to deliver a coup de grâce, Proykiev announced he is to be spared. That much is clear. But why? After sorting through the possible explanations, Kasparanov can only conclude that the General Secretary has ordered that he not be arrested. Again he asks himself, "Why?" And then it hits him!

Proykiev has the old guard who approved Kasparanov's plan, including the General Secretary, in his sights and Schnelling is the key. If Schnelling dies, the plan dies, its champions are discredited and the ruthless Proykiev, always the political grim reaper, will be well-positioned to become the head of the KGB, the next step on the path to becoming General Secretary of the Communist Party or Premier of the Soviet Union or both. Proykiev's unexpected appearance in Kasparanov's office means Schnelling is still alive, and that Schnelling has unwittingly become a key figure in the Kremlin's fierce internal politics. There is no doubt in

Kasparanov's mind that if Proykiev is elevated to the head of the KGB or, worse, the head of both the Party and the government, then nuclear war with the West, a position Proykiev has openly advocated for since 1953, is inevitable. Kasparanov has to get a message to Schnelling. Kropotkin must be eliminated or the mission will fail and the fallout from Schnelling's death could envelop the globe in a catastrophe far worse than the one he has planned and championed!

The simple calculation of this man east of the Iron Curtain is that for the sake of his country and the sake of the world, Kropotkin must die.

CHAPTER 48

A MESSAGE AND A BOTTLE

The café on Jägerstrasse in East Berlin is nearly empty. Cliff Thompson sits in a booth by himself and drinks a cup of ridiculously awful coffee at the end of an uneventful day. A modest crowd will gather for beer and potatoes over the course of the next two hours, but for now Thompson and three other men, not including the bartender, have the small place to themselves.

A construction worker enters. He still has the grime from a day's work on his thick hands and weather-beaten face. His denim overalls are dusty as are his work boots. A faded plaid shirt hangs loosely on his sturdy frame.

He catches Thompson's eye as he enters the café. Thompson waves him off with a slight nod. The worker takes his dirty felt hat off and walks towards the small bar at the back of the café. As he passes Thompson he places a small slip of folded paper next to Thompson's right hand. Thompson immediately covers the message with his hand. The worker continues to the back of the bar.

"Budvar," the worker orders. The bartender pulls a bottle of the Czech pilsner from under the bar, opens it with a church key bottle opener tied to his soiled apron, and places the open bottle on the bar.

Thompson unfolds the slip of paper to read the message. It's encrypted. Thompson pockets the message, throws a few east marks on his table, and leaves the café. He turns west out of the café and then north, heading for Unter den Linden three blocks away.

He picks out an empty bench on the south side of the wide boulevard. He sits and casually looks around to ensure he has caught no one's attention. Satisfied on that point, he pulls a pocket-sized, paperback copy of Das Kapital from the breast pocket of his light blazer. Turning modern communism's founding document into a serviceable code book satisfies his disdain for all governments, and, as always, he is unable to stifle a slight, ironic smile as he opens the book.

The decoded message is simple: "Lass Kropotkin leben." It makes no sense to him. The translation is easy enough: Let Kropotkin live. Thompson recalls Nick Temple having talked about a Soviet killing machine by the name of Kropotkin, but other than that the message is a complete mystery. Since his role is limited to that of courier, the fact that the message means nothing to him is of no import. He'll see to it that Arnie Miller gets the message and that'll be the end of it so far as he's concerned.

But Miller will have to wait. Too many cables and too many trips back and forth in too short of a time span will cause even the dullards at STASI to smell a rat. Thompson hopes the message can wait. Three more days should do it. Anything sooner invites increased scrutiny, and increased scrutiny equals unacceptable risk.

CHAPTER 49

THE MEASURE OF A MAN

Nick reviews the file from Langley one more time: Hartmut Schnelling, a despicable man who has spent nearly 20 years taking the darkest path he could find at nearly every turn. His war record is suspect enough. After the full extent of the atrocities of the Second World War came to light, the world learned to regard German scientists, however unfairly, with suspicion. In Schnelling's case, the suspicions were well-founded. His wartime "camp" activities brought him to the attention of the Nürnberg prosecutors, but his 1945 escape to the East where he curried the favor of his Soviet occupiers prevented him from being brought to justice.

He profited handsomely from the Soviets' need for skilled scientists after the intelligentsia's brutal and near-total destruction during Stalin's purges followed closely by 20 million dead in the war. The post-war expansion of the Soviet Army's chemical and biological weapons of mass destruction owed much to the efforts of Schnelling. By the late 1950s, Schnelling had reportedly defected once again and retired to an undisclosed location in the Caribbean. The reports were wrong. The Company now knows that far from retiring Schnelling went to work overseeing the discreet construction of a sophisticated laboratory to conduct experiments leading to the production of a strain of vaccine-resistant polio.

"One sick bastard," Nick thinks to himself.

Each member of the team has read the file. Now it's decision time. The team members are gathered around the veranda table of their mountainside retreat. Nick works a tall glass of iced tea. A few glasses of ice water sit on the table next to photographs of Schnelling and Kropotkin. Pete Hall sips a rum and Coke.

"It seems to me that the question is what he will do when we eliminate Kropotkin."

"If he thinks the Sovs did it, he'll fold his tent and get out of Dodge," Kyle Richardson offers.

"Take his toys and go home?" Pete Hall asks.

"Something like that, although I'm not sure where a guy like that calls home."

"And what if he correctly surmises the Americans have taken out Kropotkin?" Nick asks.

"As far as we know, it's just Schnelling and Kropotkin on the island. He's going to feel isolated and vulnerable at any rate," is Dalila's contribution.

"I've had a hard time believing there isn't more muscle around this guy, but that seems to be the case. Does that mean the Soviets might not be that invested?" Nick asks the team.

"Either that or they're keeping things low-key for a reason," Kyle counters. "It's worked for them so far. We really have no idea how long he's been working here undetected. Frankly, Nick, if you hadn't picked the island for a bit of R&R he'd never have come up on anybody's radar at least on this side of the pond."

"That's a fact. And you're right. Just because he's been working alone doesn't tell us that the Russians aren't fully committed. It's actually a smart strategy, especially for a group that tends toward overkill."

"He'll certainly go underground, at least in the near term, no matter who he thinks did it." Pete Hall has learned that his insights are valued irrespective of his lack of a background in intelligence.

"If underground's his lab, we're going to be up against it. Especially if he simply stays there until it's time to move north."

They all nod in agreement with Dalila's assessment.

Lieutenant Escobar chimes in.

"I take it we're a go on the Kropotkin sting?"

"Absolutely," is Nick's immediate response. "He's too much of a threat to our security, and his elimination could well end the mission. It's worth the risk all the way around."

"Then your question about Schnelling will answer itself. In the meantime, we should focus on tomorrow knowing that we'll just have to wait and see what Schnelling does in response."

The team's members look to Nick. He contemplates Escobar's proposal for a moment before looking up.

"You're absolutely right. Kropotkin is job one. So, let's take about a five minute break and then go over the raid one more time to see if it needs any fine tuning."

They all nod. Kyle and Pete stand up and head inside. Lieutenant Escobar approaches Nick.

"I hope I didn't step on anyone's toes."

"Absolutely not. We're in this thing together, and anything you have, or anyone else has to say, has to be on the table. Your point was solid and I'm glad you made it. Fair enough?"

"Got it."

Escobar and Guzman head inside as well, leaving Nick and Dalila alone on the veranda.

Nick takes a sip from his sweating glass of iced tea.

"Got your lines memorized?"

"To the extent I can."

"How's the dress fit?"

"It should be convincing."

"Can't wait."

Dalila flashes a sly smile at Nick before leaning in to whisper.

"I'll wear it just for you someday soon."

She finds his hand and squeezes it. He responds by pulling her to him. He whispers in return.

"Like I said, I can't wait."

CHAPTER 50

OUT OF THE FRYING PAN

Kyle Richardson once again sits on the steps of the fountain in Church Square. This time, instead of enjoying a mango, he peruses *The Virgin Islands Daily News* while keeping the stairs leading to Calypso Willy's in his peripheral vision. His Panama hat shades him from the already intense late morning sun. His short sleeve polo shirt offers no protection for his forearms and biceps now deeply tanned from his current stint in the tropics.

Nick Temple sits in the team's Jeep Utility Wagon half a block away on the opposite side of the square. A thin wire runs from a small earphone in his right ear to a transistor receiver hooked to his belt. He can't see the stairway entrance from his position, but he can see Richardson. When it's time for Escobar and Guzman to move, Nick will start the Jeep's engine, Kyle will fold his newspaper, and Escobar and Guzman will head up the stairs.

Escobar and Guzman stroll near a row of fruit stands on the south side of the square, one or both of them keeping an eye on Richardson. Each has a set of handcuffs and a fully loaded M1911 .45 caliber semiautomatic pistol tucked into his waistband and concealed by a loose-fitting shirt.

One of the St. Thomas Department of Public Safety's aging patrol cars, a two-door 1950 Ford purchased eight years ago from the Miami P.D., is parked along the street just north of the stairway entrance. As prearranged, at 11:15 the patrol car pulls away. The Department's Police

Division temporarily cedes de facto authority over the area of operations to Nick and his team.

At a sidewalk café two blocks north of the square, Pete Hall sits alone at a small table, reads the latest issue of *National Geographic*, and nurses a flat Coke. A large umbrella protects him from the climbing sun. He checks his watch. If all goes according to Kropotkin's foolishly established schedule, Dalila should be out of Calypso Willy's and safely at the café before 11:30.

Team Temple is in place.

Less than five minutes later Kropotkin strolls to the square from the waterfront side. Looking like a man without a care, he turns right into the stairway and bounds up the stairs.

Dalila Atieno sits on a bar stool behind a small reception desk that poorly guards the entrance to Calypso Willy's. Behind her, separated by no more than two meters of wall, are two doorways. The doorway to her right as she sits at the desk leads to Willy's bar and pool tables. The other doorway leads to a corridor lined by three small, unadorned bedrooms on each side. The keys for the corridor's rooms hang on eye hooks directly behind Dalila. The hallway is the target of Kropotkin's habitual visits.

Dalila sits in her red, flower print, sleeveless dress and casually leafs through a story about American Westerns in an issue of *Look* magazine from earlier that year. She wears red flats to facilitate movement in the event speed is necessary. To Dalila's front is a small sitting area with two cushioned rattan chairs each of which is occupied by a languid prostitute from Santo Domingo. One files her nails; the other fans herself; both are oblivious to what is about to take place.

Kropotkin walks in. Dalila knows he has entered but she continues to leaf through the magazine, feigning ennui.

"Hey! You have customer. Wake up."

Dalila slowly looks up from her magazine. Kropotkin is huge and far more menacing in person than in his photographs. She does her best to maintain her composure as she pulls a cheap guest register from the top shelf under the desk and flops it carelessly on the counter. She opens to the day's date, takes a ballpoint pen from a jar on the counter, and sets the pen on the open register.

"Sign in."

She turns to grab a key to room 5, the one Kyle wired for sound yesterday.

"Sign in? Where is usual girl? I don't sign in. Don't they tell you?"

Dalila turns around to face Kropotkin.

"Okay. Sign in. Don't sign in. Your choice."

She grabs a towel from the bottom shelf of the reception desk and places it, with the key on top of it, on the desktop.

"Number 5. On the left. Ten dollars American in advance."

Dalila puts her elbow on the desk and casually holds her hand out waiting to be paid.

Kropotkin pulls a folded ten dollar bill out of his shirt pocket and slams it on the desk top.

"Next time I pay in rubles!" He laughs at his own joke, grabs the towel and key, and heads down the hallway.

Nick hears the door to room number 5 open. The reception is perfect.

"You again?" he hears Kropotkin complain.

"You hurt the other girls too much," is the poor woman's response.

"Ha! They don't know what real pain is. I will teach you and you can teach them," Kropotkin threatens.

Nick shakes his head and thinks to himself, "This sick fuck never lets up."

Through his earpiece he can hear the sounds of Kropotkin undressing. Within moments the creaking of an old, well-worn spring mattress takes over. Time to move.

Nick starts the Jeep's engine; Kyle hears the engine turnover and immediately folds his newspaper; Escobar and Guzman bolt from the fruit stand, race to the stairwell and are in Calypso Willy's less than 20 seconds after Nick's initial signal. With their weapons drawn they head down the corridor of rooms.

Dalila comes out from behind the counter.

"Time to go, ladies," she urges the two prostitutes.

Alarmed by the presence of armed men they offer no resistance and follow Dalila. The three women quickly make their way to the square where Dalila turns north to find Pete Hall and her ride back to the team's quarters.

Back in Calypso Willy's, Escobar and Guzman halt outside the closed door to room number 5. They listen for a moment to make sure Kropotkin is still occupied. Escobar looks at Guzman and signals the count of three. The instant Escobar reaches "three," Guzman smashes the door open by delivering a swift kick to its flimsy doorknob. Both men rush in.

The prostitute, lying on her back, screams. The naked Kropotkin, turns to see the two men and springs from the bed for his pile of clothes. Guzman delivers an uppercut to Kropotkin's jaw with his fist and pistol sending Kropotkin flying back onto the bed. Guzman sees the Makarov Kropotkin was diving for and grabs it.

The prostitute, still screaming, flees the room wrapped in the bed's lone sheet. Kropotkin recovers almost instantly from Guzman's blow and lunges at Escobar. Escobar fires at Kropotkin's thigh stopping him dead in his tracks. Another blow to the back of the head from Guzman's pistol grip renders the wounded Kropotkin briefly unconscious in a heap on the floor next to the bed.

Escobar and Guzman roll the enormous Russian over on his face, pull his hands behind his back and handcuff him. Guzman grabs the pitcher of water from the small dresser opposite the bed and empties it on Kropotkin's head, reviving him.

"Turn over!" Escobar commands.

Guzman grabs Kropotkin's shoulder and helps Kropotkin turn over. The wound to his thigh is severe. Guzman knows Kropotkin doesn't have long to live. Still, he rips Kropotkin's shirt, fashions a tourniquet, and ties it tightly around the bleeding thigh.

Kropotkin tries to head butt Guzman just as Guzman is finishing, but he manages only a glancing blow. Escobar kicks Kropotkin's thigh at the point of the wound and sends Kropotkin into spasms of pain.

Guzman gets behind Kropotkin, grabs him under the armpits, and stands him up.

"Let's go."

With Guzman's pistol held fast against Kropotkin's temple, the two MPs drag the naked and wounded Kropotkin, who tries to keep up by hopping on his one good leg, out into the hallway, through the reception area, to the stairway and down to the street.

Nick Temple and Kyle Richardson wait in the Jeep at the curb in front of the stairway. Richardson hops out, opens the right, rear door of the Jeep and helps Escobar and Guzman stuff the struggling Kropotkin into the back seat. As soon as Kropotkin is in he looks up and sees Nick Temple behind the wheel.

"Temple! Malenkov should have let me kill you in Berlin."

"Too late, you piece of shit."

Richardson jumps in the front passenger seat and Guzman climbs in next to Kropotkin. Escobar heads for the Rambler parked a block west of the square. Nick speeds away from the curb.

Guzman, weapon drawn and pointed at Kropotkin's head, tells Kropotkin to get down. He refuses. Guzman grinds the nose of his weapon against Kropotkin's wound.

"How about now?"

Kropotkin groans and writhes in pain before he finally relents, twisting his massive frame into the fetal position in the left half of the Jeep's back seat.

The sandy road leads to a small, shaded spot used as a parking lot by the occasional visitor to the beach west of Coki Point. Nick pulls in. Right behind him is Escobar in the Rambler with its top up. The lot and beach are otherwise empty. Nick stops and motions to Guzman and Richardson to get out. They get out and immediately climb into the Rambler. Nick turns to address Kropotkin.

"How's your memory, Kropotkin?"

Kropotkin, weak from blood loss, doesn't answer.

"Vanessa Porter. The name mean anything to you?"

Kropotkin responds weakly.

"One of Malenkov's whores. Do you want to know what she said right before I slit her throat?"

"Fuck you."

"Right! A tough bitch."

Kropotkin, his mouth a mess of blood and broken teeth, finds the strength to let out a deep, guttural laugh.

Nick gets out of the car and slams the door. Kropotkin writhes and yells as he struggles one last time to free himself and escape from the car. Nick gets into the back seat of the Rambler. Escobar pulls out of the lot and drives west down the narrow sandy road away from the beach. Nick keeps his eyes on the Jeep from the back seat to make sure Kropotkin doesn't escape.

After the Rambler travels about 50 meters, Nick says simply, "Okay."

Richardson pulls a small, 3-channel walkie-talkie out of the glove compartment, switches it on, and tunes it to one of the fixed frequencies.

"Dosvidaniya, asshole."

He presses the push-to-talk button.

Nick shields his eyes from a bright flash followed by an enormous blast as the Jeep and Kropotkin are blown to small bits of metal, rubber, glass, bone, and flesh. Kropotkin's hands and severed forearms, still linked together by Lieutenant Escobar's handcuffs, tumble grotesquely through the air in a graceful arc until they land on a beach that just moments before could have been mistaken for paradise.

CHAPTER 51

A DAY LATE AND A DOLLAR SHORT

The news of Kropotkin's death flows quickly back to the Cold War centers of power.

Proykiev reads a copy of the encoded cable. He reads it half a dozen times before he can no longer tell himself that he is misinterpreting its message. He sits back in his office chair for a moment with his hands folded on his lap. He exhales, stands, and walks to his fourth-story office window for a breath of fresh air. The window consists of two panes that open outward stretching from a sill less than a meter above the floor all the way to the ceiling. He opens the window by slowly rotating a crank at the base of the right pane clockwise until both panes are perpendicular to the building's outer wall. He steps up to stand on the sill and immediately, almost mechanically, spills out of the window ending his life with a thud on the sidewalk below.

The General Secretary rubs his temples as he rereads the messages in front of him. Proykiev's gamble has failed. The Americans have eliminated Kropotkin leaving no one in place to terminate the German. They should have left Kropotkin alone. Kasparanov and the old guard will be able to breathe easier. The Army and Navy will undoubtedly continue to insist that the Cuba initiative, now being called Operation Anadyr, proceed on the fantastic assumption that a nuclear contest with the Americans is winnable. Only time will tell if he and others who are like-minded will be able to pull the nation back from that brink. And if the German succeeds, the end may come sooner rather than later.

Arnie Miller gets two messages nearly simultaneously. The first, from Cliff Thompson, is simple and clear: Let Kropotkin live. He is about to relay that message across the pond when Terry enters his office with the second message, this one from Langley. The second message is equally simple and clear: Kropotkin terminated Caribbean sector. He rereads the second message before looking up at his secretary.

"I need to get ahold of Bill Johnson."

The Director scans his daily briefing. As has been his habit for years, he also peruses the previous day's European cable traffic while he drinks his second cup of morning coffee. He is looking for any sign of a reaction from the Warsaw Pact nations to Kropotkin's death. He can only wait and see if the sanction, undertaken on the assumption that Schnelling will abandon his efforts with Kropotkin's elimination, will have the desired effect. The only item that catches his eye is an encrypted transmission from one of Langley's own, an assistant to the Chargé d'Affaires in Moscow, reporting the suicide of the Deputy Commissar of the KGB's First Chief Directorate.

CHAPTER 52

DAMAGE CONTROL

A heavy summer rain that began earlier in the afternoon continues to drench St. Thomas well past dark. With the rain beating down around them, team Temple gathers in the musty living room of their quarters recovering from the news of a gross miscalculation on their part. Arnie Miller's message via Langley confirmed that someone in the upper echelon of the Soviet political command structure, for whatever reason, wanted a man sent to protect a key component of a frightening new capability dead. Nick and his team did some top-ranking Commie a big fat favor! They don't know who, and they don't know why, but the intel is solid. Cliff Thompson's warning was delivered too late to be actionable, and now Nick and his team are wondering what's next – not a good feeling for intel types.

Kyle reads the message from Langley one more time before tossing it on the coffee table.

"What the hell is Moscow up to?"

"There's got to be some sort of wrestling match going on inside the Kremlin. The sad fact is that by terminating Kropotkin we cozied up to one side without knowing who it is or what they're after."

"He was going to shut Schnelling down," Dalila declares.

"It looks that way," Nick agrees.

"Or at least remove him from the process," Kyle adds.

"Why can't we finish what Kropotkin left undone?" Pete Hall asks.

"It's one thing to take out a KGB thug who's on American soil illegally; it's another to go randomly execute an East German citizen who's a long-time territorial resident. All of that license to kill bullshit is just that – bullshit. It doesn't exist. Besides, we need him to take us to his lab."

After a moment of nervous silence, Dalila asks, "What are our options at this point?"

"We stay focused on finding the lab and destroying it," Nick announces matter-of-factly.

"Good old fashioned police work is the key," Escobar observes.

"Can you stick around for a while longer? We could definitely use the two of you."

"I'll make some calls. I don't think it should be a problem, but Langley's going to have to foot the bill."

"I'll take care of that," Nick responds.

"Well, hell. No sense sitting around kicking ourselves over this thing. Kropotkin's dead. I for one won't miss him. Maybe he would have done our work for us, maybe not. Now it doesn't matter. The simple fact is that we haven't completed what we came here to do, and we need to figure out how we're going to do that as quickly as possible."

"Kyle's right, of course. We don't know how much time we have, so we should assume that time is of the essence. Let's call it a night unless anyone has any bright ideas they want to put on the table right now."

"Surveillance," Guzman interjects.

"Absolutely."

"We haven't done anything to work the locals," Kyle adds. "The lab didn't just pop up out of nowhere. There are people on this island who had a hand in putting that thing together."

"More straight-forward police work," Guzman replies.

"No need to be coy about it. Schnelling and the Russians know we're here."

"You think so, Nick?" Kyle asks with a sly smile.

They all laugh.

"Tough even for the Russians to ignore the message. Naked, hand-cuffed, and blown to bits. Nice bit of payback," he adds.

"Yeah. I guess we weren't exactly subtle. I've been thinking about that moment for about four years."

"Should have taken out an ad," Pete Hall interjects.

"Did you see yesterday's paper?" Dalila asks.

"Yeah, but does it count as an ad when you don't pay for it?" Pete responds, eliciting laughter from the rest of the team.

Nick, seeing that the team's mood has improved, takes the opportunity to end the evening on that note.

"I'll let the folks at DPS know that we'll be working the problem on the streets. Government House may be able to help us out there. Raoul, I'm going to ask you to put together a plan. It seems to me we're in local investigation mode for the time being which is right up your alley."

"At your service. We'll go over it first thing in the morning."

"That's settled then. Let's turn in. We've got a lot of work ahead of us. We'll hit it hard tomorrow."

They all agree. While the sense of poor execution lingers, no one in the group is anything but resolute about their ultimate goal: Schnelling and his engineered polio virus must be stopped.

CHAPTER 53

CULTURE SHOCK

"You drive."

"I can't read the signs."

"Just follow the others."

"And if we're separated, what then, Yuri?"

"In that case you can just keep driving until we get back to Romny."

"And leave this workers' paradise?"

"I prefer a workers' paradise where the workers can at least read the road signs."

"So you see my point."

"I do. Unfortunately, I do."

"Which means you have to drive."

Dmitri Bogdonevitch and Yuri Belyavski, not unlike the other men of the second regiment of the 43rd Guards Rocket Division, are having more than a little difficulty adjusting to their new surroundings.

At first, after word of their destination filtered down to them two days sail out of Sevastopol, they talked of nothing but what they supposed life in the tropics under a Havana moon would hold for them. As they steamed west they imagined tropical fruit drinks spiked with rum; white sand beaches mobbed by scantily-clad Cuban women welcoming the men serving the vanguard of Socialism; the slow pace and old world charm of a former capitalist colony; and an ethic well-suited to their unofficial motto of "They pretend to pay us, and we pretend to work."

Instead they have encountered relentless heat, swarms of mosquitoes and other flying, biting things, a suspicious if not outright hostile local population, and a work schedule that is brutal by anyone's standards. They are up before dawn and spend every day working like madmen to prepare launch sites and equipment to render their unit's weapons operational.

Like soldiers all over the world and since the beginning of time, the men of the 43rd Guards Rocket Division complain. Like good Russian soldiers their complaints are laced with a healthy dose of irreverent humor. But beneath the complaints, beneath the humor runs a current of incredulity. Each man struggles to comprehend what they know to be the truth: they are moving the world's two foremost nuclear superpowers rapidly towards a confrontation that could easily result in the end of life on earth as they know it.

CHAPTER 54

TARGET ACQUISITION

The Director skims the executive summary one more time. Across from him sits the Army's premier expert on the Soviet Union's military capabilities and Warsaw Pact strategy, Colonel Stan Stratton.

"Cuba? We're sure? I know we've been getting some wild reports from the expats in Miami, and most of it's garbage."

"U-2 reconnaissance confirms it, sir."

"The President and the Joint Chiefs?"

"Being informed as we speak, sir."

Stratton, currently attached to the National Security Agency, hands the Director another manila file marked TOP SECRET.

"Copies of the flyover aerial photographs are in the file, sir, along with shipping routes, known tonnage, and aerial photographs of merchant marine activity from the Navy. You'll note in the Navy's photographs that the waterlines on the merchant marine ships are right at surface level. Those ships are fully loaded."

The Director leafs through the report quickly.

"That's a hell of a lot of hardware. How solid are those numbers?"

"The numbers are our best judgment based upon site preparation from the flyovers, unit redeployment activity in the Soyuz, HUMINT out of Cuba, SIGINT from Key West, and transoceanic maritime traffic from Sevastopol, Vladivostok, Suez, Gibraltar, and Panama, as determined from sources on the ground and aerial photographic evidence. Needless to say, we've had our best people on it."

"Payloads?"

"Same answer, sir."

"What's our vulnerability?"

"Once they're operational, extensive to say the least. We've included a map in the materials as Appendix C."

The Director flips through the file until coming to Appendix C; its import is immediately apparent.

"Just about the whole damn country."

"Yes, sir."

"What's your best judgment? Are they bluffing?"

"I think we should assume they're not, sir. The sheer scope of the operation is too extensive to reasonably constitute a feint. If it's a bluff, it's a costly one."

"Which may be exactly what they want us to think. Their huge operation forces us to pour everything we've got into a response on Cuba. Meanwhile they're shoving it to us on the other side of the globe while everyone on this side of the Iron Curtain's losing their collective sanity over a nuclear conflict that's never going to happen."

"Always a possibility, sir, although in my judgment it sounds too imaginative for their current leadership. And the risk for the West of being wrong about such a possibility is simply not supportable."

"What about the next level, just below the big shots?"

The intercom on the Director's desk buzzes before the Colonel can answer.

"Excuse me, Colonel."

The Director flips a switch on the intercom.

"What is it, Cheryl?"

"Your presence is required at the White House in an hour, sir, for an emergency meeting of the NSC."

"Thanks, Cheryl. Let my driver know. I'll be ready in five minutes."

He flips the switch to off.

"Are you part of this briefing, Colonel?"

"I am, sir. The President is forming a special group to respond to the crisis."

"You can ride with me and we'll talk on the way. There's another Caribbean operation this may affect."

"Temple's outfit?"

"You know about it. Good. I want to talk about the possibility of linkage between Cuba and St. Thomas. Are there any strategic or tactical connections, or are we just looking at a coincidence? Does Ivan's left hand know what his right hand is doing?"

"Without knowing where the orders are coming from on the St. Thomas matter, it's difficult to say, sir."

"Wouldn't they be coming from the top?"

"The logistics, as I understand them, are limited enough that the operation could conceivably have been initiated at some intermediate level, just below the big shots, as you put it. But again, it's difficult to say for certain."

"Well, Colonel, we get paid to make the difficult calls. When you get back to the shop, I want you and your boys to assume they're connected and see if any evidence under analysis supports that assumption."

"With all due respect, sir, I'm working non-stop on the missiles in Cuba as of two days ago. That's directly from General Blake."

"Understood. I'll chat with your boss after the NSC meeting. If I can't get him to pull you away for a few hours, I want you to at least keep that possibility in the back of your mind as you go through the intel. Can you do that much for me?"

"Certainly can, sir."

"Thanks. And I'll keep the Old Man in the loop."

"Probably best."

The Director grabs the TOP SECRET file off his desk, stands, and comes out from behind his desk.

"Let's get going. My car should be waiting."

The Director opens his office door allowing Colonel Stratton to exit ahead of him. They leave Langley not knowing for certain if what America's intelligence community has uncovered is the dreaded "beginning of the end," merely another infuriating bit of Soviet brinksmanship, or an elaborate piece of theater conjured up solely for its ability to occupy the complete attention of America's leaders while some other operation unfolds undetected and unopposed.

CHAPTER 55

NO MORE HOUSECALLS

Hartmut Schnelling cannot believe his good fortune. The Americans could not have done him any greater service. The turnaround since Kropotkin's death has been remarkable. Encrypted wire communications with Moscow have been restored, the operation is to proceed as originally conceived, and his own freedom of action is no longer hampered by the Russian's hulking presence.

The lack of activity anywhere near his lab is a clear sign that the Americans have no idea where it is. And while he assumes they are aware of his presence and identity, before noon today he will have moved himself to the lab for the duration of the production process, not reappearing again until hours before arranging for shipment to the American mainland and leaving St. Thomas for good six days hence.

It is barely dawn as he runs through his brief supply checklist one more time: five gallons of gasoline for the emergency generator; four spare 2.4 volt batteries for the R-104M radio at the lab; ten fully loaded 30-round magazines of 7.62x39mm cartridges for the AK-47 at the lab; one additional ammo box of one thousand rounds; four thermite grenades for equipment and records destruction as he abandons the lab; food and fresh water for up to ten days; first aid kit; adequate clothing and personal hygiene items for the duration.

As he finishes the list he can't help laughing to himself. The man who is about to unleash history's worst attack by a foreign enemy on American soil is counting rolls of toilet paper! Now that his personal safety appears to have been secured by the unwitting Americans he reflects with some personal pride on his meticulous preparation. If the mission fails, it will not be due to lack of discipline and dedication on his part.

Having already moved the heaviest necessities–ammunition, water, and gasoline–to the lab, he moves the rest of the items on his check list from his kitchen table to his Volvo station wagon parked directly in front of his modest bungalow. The humid early morning after a tropical downpour presages a sweltering day. And Hartmut Schnelling, with the wind now at his back, looks forward to a week in the tropics as he never has before.

CHAPTER 56

THE OLD FASHIONED WAY

Since the operation for the moment has become a straight-forward police investigation, Nick has handed over the reins to the best cop on the team, Lieutenant Escobar. The downpour stopped during the early morning allowing the team to gather on the still damp veranda as they finish their morning coffee.

"Sergeant Guzman and I will work the suppliers. Building materials, hardware, generators, etc. Dr. Hall, I think you should work the science side of the operation. Where would he get what he needs to conduct his work? What does he need? What quantities does he need? Who might supply those materials? What assistance would he need in setting up the lab? Cast as broad a net initially as possible. Pharmacies, hospitals, personnel being recruited for the new college, government agencies, any place that might include a scientist with a need for, and access to materials."

"Got it," is Pete's confident response.

"Nick, head over to the professor's house. If it looks like he's still there, stake it out and follow him if he leaves. We might get lucky, but I think it's a safe bet that he's already headed to the lab for the duration. If it looks like he's checked out, head over to Government House and see if you can't get us some help on the transportation side. It's going to take some tedious document review. We're looking at shipping traffic, customs logs, quarantine logs, anything unusual that our professor may have had to custom order and ship. Who got that order? Where did they deliver it? When?"

"I'll take care of it."

"Dalila and Kyle, see what you can find out from the local labor force. Concentrate on day laborers. If St. Thomas is anything like San Juan, there will be informal pick-up spots in town, places where men congregate hoping to get a day's work. Find out where those places are. Talk to the men. See if any of them worked for Schnelling, helped him with the lab, or have heard rumors of other groups of workers being used on the lab. We're a couple of years behind, but it's still worth looking into.

"Okay, that should get us started. We'll meet back here this evening to see what we have, what's worth following up on, and what we can eliminate. Questions?"

Lieutenant Escobar grabs his coffee mug and takes a gulp. Nick is the first to speak up.

"Nice work, Raoul. It looks pretty straight forward. I just want to add that we should try to keep this as low key as possible for the moment. If you run into any resistance, if anyone gets their hackles up, back off. We don't want to spook the professor if we can help it."

Kyle can't help ribbing Nick, so he asks, "If I read you right, you're saying don't blow anyone to bits on a beach?"

Nick smiles as he responds. "Yeah, I think that's a good rule of thumb. But, if push comes to shove, do what you have to do. That's it, then. Back here by six this evening."

CHAPTER 57

PEERING OVER THE BRINK

Just a few days ago Yevgeny Kasparanov thought he would never see the inside of this office again, that a cell in the basement of the Lubyanka would be his new address until a suitable work camp in Siberia was found. Instead, Proykiev is dead, the St. Thomas operation is back in full swing, and he is meeting with the General Secretary to discuss the progress of Operation Anadyr. Just another day on the roller coaster that is political life in the Soviet Union.

"You've had an eventful week, Yevgeny Nikolaievitch."

"To say the least."

"And now the world will have an eventful month."

"What progress is there on Cuba?"

"Our tactical progress is something we should all be quite proud of. Your plan has been executed nearly flawlessly. There have been problems with some of the launch sites, but we've been able to find suitable alternatives in short order preserving our target capabilities. It's quite remarkable, really."

"And once all is in place?"

"Ah, that is now the question that few dare to utter. How is it you are so bold?"

"I feel certain I speak with a man who shares my point of view."

"That may be so, but the hardliners may yet have their way."

"Where are the Americans?"

"We've heard nothing yet. We have to assume a level of reconnaissance that is likely putting the entire matter squarely before them, but we do not know how much they have detected. There is the small team on St. Thomas. The ones who did your bidding."

"An amazing turn of events."

"They'll turn their attention to your professor now."

"Undoubtedly, but he is at least a step ahead of them."

"He has a remarkable capacity for survival."

"And if he succeeds where Anadyr cannot?"

"I should think their leadership would be relieved. It may cause terror among the people, but this, after all is our goal, is it not?"

"Success for Schnelling equals leverage for our country around the world."

"Or American fury."

"A calculated risk, but one that does not involve nuclear weapons."

"I hope we're right about that."

The General Secretary pauses. The view of the West that this man is a simple, blustering peasant is one he carefully cultivates. In reality he is as comfortable in the world of seemingly disjointed abstract thought as he is in the world of blatantly crude application of naked power. And at times he considers himself the lone voice of reason among a group of leaders characterized by a dangerous mix of paranoia, megalomania, and a penchant for intrigue. But so long as he remains in power, he feels certain he can engineer a return from the looming nuclear brink with the Americans. What they'll do in response to a biological attack on their homeland is quite another matter. There is no precedent upon which to draw to gauge their potential reaction. Pearl Harbor? By 1962 it's almost quaint to think in terms of conventional warfare.

"And how is your young family, my friend?"

"We are all well, as well as one can be in these uncertain times."

"You should spend more time with them."

"My wife understands, but I'm afraid I'm practically a stranger to my daughter."

"Go home. The world will turn without you for a day or so. There will be plenty to do later in the week. For now, we can't do much more than wait. So go home, tend to your family. Rest for the days ahead."

Yevgeny Kasparanov, delighted to be once again in the obvious good graces of the man who, for the moment, is the single most powerful man in the Soviet Union, stands and offers his hand to the General Secretary.

"Thank you. I will."

They shake hands. Kasparanov leaves, and the General Secretary returns to contemplating the enormous map of the world adorning the entire west wall of his outsized office.

CHAPTER 58

ALL IN A DAY'S WORK

Nick Temple, behind the wheel of a newly-purchased Jeep Station Wagon, pulls up about 20 meters down the street from the home of Hartmut Schnelling. The Director, knowing that Uncle Sam would likely end up "buying the damn thing," as he put it, authorized Nick to use one of the U.S. Treasury drafts in his possession to purchase the Jeep. The transaction raised a few eyebrows at the dealership, but paying the full sticker price helped grease the skids.

Nick parks on the opposite side of the quiet, shady lane, turns off the ignition, and settles in to watch. He checks his Bulova Sunburst: 8:17 a.m.

Within minutes, an islander in his early thirties approaches Schnelling's house on the sidewalk across from where Nick is parked. He is dressed casually: loose fitting khakis, a white, short-sleeved sport shirt, and white Spring Court tennis shoes. A bulky, black canvas bag is slung over his left shoulder. He surprises Nick by turning at the small sidewalk leading to Schnelling's house.

"I guess we'll find out if Schnelling is in," Nick thinks to himself.

The man stops at the front door. Instead of knocking he pulls a key out of his pants pocket, slips it into the doorknob, turns it, looks quickly around, and enters the house, closing the door behind him.

Nick waits 30 seconds before getting out of the Jeep. He silently closes the car door and crosses the deserted street. He approaches the house but leaves the sidewalk about three meters before reaching the property line. He walks to the side of the house towards a small front room window. He stops before reaching the window and, with his back pressed against the house's outside wall, peers into the living room. A thin, gauze curtain obscures most of his view of the room. By crouching and positioning himself on the other side of the window he is able to make out the main features of the room through a break between the curtain and the wall.

He sees the man who entered the house on his knees in the middle of the living room. He's emptying his black bag. Plastic explosives! C-4, and lots of it, detonators, and trip wires. He's booby-trapping the house. Nick guesses that this is the same man responsible for wrecking his day of novice surfing and ending a hapless thief's life a few months back. Schnelling has probably moved out and is taking one more shot at Nick, assuming he'll break into the house once it's clear Schnelling isn't returning.

The man finishes placing the explosives in an arc around the front door threshold. He works on setting a trip wire just inside the door. Any movement of the door will detonate the impressive load of C-4 creating a kill zone with a diameter of at least ten meters.

Nick heads to the cottage's back door, the only exit the man has left himself. He places himself flat against the house next to the door and waits.

Less than two minutes later the back door opens inward slightly. The man who set the explosives peers out from inside the house. He puts the fingers of his right hand against the door's threshold as he prepares to check to see if his exit will be detected. Nick sees his chance. He grabs the doorknob and pulls the door shut on the man's fingers. He then turns and kicks the door which smashes into the man's face. Nick's victim cries out in pain trying to decide whether to grab his broken fingers or his broken nose. He stumbles blindly back into the house's small kitchen falling to the floor after backing into a chair. He screams in pain once again as he tries to brace his fall with his smashed hand.

Nick jumps into the kitchen and closes the back door behind him. With his Beretta drawn, he pounces on the man and sticks the barrel of the pistol against the man's cheek.

"Nice try, asshole. Where's Schnelling?"

The would-be bomber writhes and groans in pain.

"What? Shit! I don't know any Schnelling! Are you fucking crazy, man?"

"Wrong answer. You've got about ten seconds to come up with the right answer or die. Your choice. Got it?"

"I just get paid to do a job. That's all I know."

"You just wasted five seconds of your life."

"All right! All right!" the man screams. "Don't shoot."

"Talk."

"He's gone. He thought you'd come around, so he paid me to have a little surprise for you when you did. I swear I don't know where he is. I've only ever met him once."

"Gone? Off the island?"

"I don't know. Just not here anymore."

"When's the last time you talked to him?"

"Yesterday, when the wire transfer was confirmed. He said he'd be out by dawn this morning and that I was to complete the job before noon."

Nick looks around the kitchen and grabs a dishrag folded on the edge of the sink. He tosses it to the man.

"For your nose."

The man uses the rag to staunch his bleeding.

Nick takes two steps towards a telephone sitting on a sideboard next to the stove. He picks up the receiver and dials.

"Operator, get me the police. Yes, it's an emergency. . . . Department of Public Safety? . . . This is Nick Temple. I've got someone here you might be interested in. . . . Check with your boss. He'll confirm. . . . Sure, I'll hold."

Nick puts his hand over the mouthpiece.

"How's the nose?"

"Go fuck yourself, man."

"Is that anyway to treat a guy you tried to kill twice?"

Nick returns to the phone conversation.

"Right. Still here. . . . Perfect. I'll wait till someone arrives. And tell whoever's coming to come in through the back. The front door's wired with about four kilos of explosives. . . . Ten minutes? Good. We'll be here."

Nick hangs up and walks over to where the man is now sitting on the floor, holding the dishrag to his nose with his one good hand. He squats down with his Beretta pointed at the man's still bleeding nose.

"Looks like your bombing days are through, buddy. We've got a nice stateside cell waiting for you. On the bright side, there's no need to fret about your future. It's all mapped out. Take a look around and enjoy, because the next time you're looking at something other than the inside of a prison you'll be in a casket."

CHAPTER 59

CRAWLING BEFORE WALKING

"Three sources confirm it. It's on the north side of the island, near the water, built almost two years ago."

Lieutenant Escobar takes a bite out of his grilled steak after that pronouncement.

"None of it's first hand," Kyle points out.

"That's not unusual given the passage of time," Guzman offers.

"The labor population is transient and seasonal. If nothing's in the works, they move on, usually to another island. We're lucky we got what we did."

"Dalila was great. Once we found the pick-up points it was all up to her. I guess I look too much like a fed."

"Isn't that what you are?" Dalila teases.

"Yeah. I thought about being the bull in a china shop and just announcing that Uncle Sam has sent the CIA down this way to clear up some nasty shit and all you motherfuckers had better start talkin', but Dalila talked me out of it."

"What's your saying? You can catch more flies with honey than vinegar?" she asks.

"She's a natural, Nick. We ought to see if we can get her on board on a permanent basis."

"I'll see what I can do. How about you, Pete? Any luck?"

"Nothing but rumblings, rumors, and not much else. The local pharmacists weren't any help, but a glass supply company on the east end seems pretty cheesed off that they didn't get a call to supply any equipment for the lab. So far as I can tell, the lab's sort of an open secret. No one knows what the guy is doing, but once word got out that he needed equipment, some of the locals who could have provided the goods tried to stick their noses in. The professor kept things pretty close to his chest. That was about two years ago, like you said, Raoul, but they're still not happy about it."

"Any luck at Government House, Nick?"

"After turning Schnelling's beat up bomber over to the locals I headed over there. I pulled all customs docs for the last three years and worked backwards. It's quite a pile. I looked for German surnames, typical German handwriting on bills of lading, anything that might tie Schnelling to an importer, supplier, shipper, or wholesaler. I didn't get through the whole pile, but as of about 24 months ago, again working backwards, only one item stood out. He must have gotten whatever else he needed offshore. I'm betting he smuggled in what he needed from Cuba. It's not like customs has this place wrapped up tight. A couple days by water from Santiago on the eastern end of Cuba via Haiti or the Dominican would be easy enough to pull off."

"You mentioned something that stood out?" Raoul asks.

"Right. A customs document that cleared six two-liter steel tanks from a German manufacturer."

"Lab equipment?"

"I don't think so."

"Pete?"

"If they can be pressurized, then he's probably planning on airborne dispersal of the formula."

"Will that work?"

"In the short term, yes. No question, particularly if he releases it into a crowd. It's the perfect vector."

The team looks to Nick.

"That's it, then. It's simple. Those tanks can't leave this island. Anything else you need from me Raoul?"

"See if you can't get us some help from the Coast Guard or the Navy scouring the north side from the water. And we need detailed maps of the bays on the north side and whatever population centers there are. The location has to be remote but accessible from the water. We'll take a look at the maps in the morning and narrow our focus."

Nick checks his watch and stands up.

"There should still be someone at Government House. I'll head down there and get the ball rolling on the extra help. They should have the maps we need, too."

"I'm coming with you. Let me get changed. This will only take a second."

Dalila heads to her bedroom. The other men look at Nick. He tries to ignore them, but relents.

"Anyone else want to ride along?"

"Need a chaperone?" Kyle asks.

"You mean a Boy Scout?"

"Just asking. Johnson's not here to keep you in line, so someone's got to take up the slack."

"I'll tell him about the great job you're doing when I talk to him."

"Okay, Nick. Seriously though, take care of her. She's one of a kind."

"You're preaching to the choir, my friend."

Dalila, wearing the dress from the Kropotkin sting, comes out of her room with a purple orchid in her hair just above her right ear and a large woven-grass shoulder bag. She has effortlessly transformed her classic African beauty into a timeless expression of tropical radiance.

"I'm ready, Mr. Temple."

"You look lovely, Dalila, far too lovely for the night shift at Government House."

"I thought I might be able to talk you into a late dinner."

"Done. Shall we?"

Nick and Dalila leave. Kyle looks around at his teammates. Guzman and Escobar shrug.

"Am I missing something?" Pete Hall asks.

"Beautiful women and Nick don't mix," Kyle explains.

"Really? That surprises me."

"An ugly divorce, an affair with a double agent, and two gruesome deaths. Dalila's up against some tough odds."

"She seems like she can handle herself."

"When he's in the field he's a target, and that makes her a target. Comes with the territory. Let's forget about it. Who needs a drink?"

Pete Hall gets up to help.

"I do. Maybe more than one."

The prospect that his newest friends might meet an ugly, violent end is a little more than Pete can take at the moment. As excited as he was at the prospect of being part of a CIA operation, the cold brutality of the Kropotkin sanction let him know that what is a fact of life for these men is frankly unfathomable for nearly all of the millions of men and women whose security is their responsibility.

CHAPTER 60

A ROOM WITH A VIEW

"Request denied. You're on your own, Nick."

"With all due respect, sir, I think you're making a mistake."

"Given what we know about what Ivan's up to in Cuba, there simply aren't any resources to reallocate. Cuba is everyone's top priority. Hell, it's our only priority for the duration whether that's a good idea or not."

"Understood."

"Sorry it has to be that way, Nick."

"Not your fault, sir. We'll take care of business here. You may see a boat and a car or two on the final tab for this op."

"Cash we can spare, but that's about it. Still have the Treasury checks?"

"I do, and I'll take that as preapproval."

"Fair enough. I trust your judgment."

"Thanks for that. By the way, the next time you see Bill Johnson tell him Kyle's taken over his spot as my personal conscience."

"Glad to hear someone's doing it. Keep me in the loop, Nick."

"I'll do it, sir. I get the feeling things are about to heat up down here, so we may be out of contact for a while. If that's the case, not to worry."

The Director laughs.

"Worry? Hell, we're only looking at nuclear war here. Who's got time to worry? Out here."

Nick hangs up the secure line and turns to Dalila.

"You catch the gist of that?"

"Only that we're not going to get any help. Did he explain why?"

"It seems the Sovs are loading up on nuclear hardware about 90 miles from Florida, as they like to say. It's got everyone on a hair trigger. Huge surprise. Everything from Alaska south is on alert or about to go on alert. In short, the country's assets are otherwise engaged for the moment."

"Sometimes less is more."

"It's certainly easier to control, and in our case, it is what it is. We'll just have to make do. Let's throw these maps in the Jeep and get some dinner. I know just the place."

The restaurant on Mafolie Hill overlooks Charlotte Amalie and its harbor to the south. The restaurant itself is not much more than a wide, covered gallery open on three sides to spectacular views below. The fare is simple; the entire menu is hand-painted onto the side of a small ceramic bottle that also serves as a vase for fresh tropical flowers on each of the restaurant's 15 tables. As the evening darkens, the only light in the restaurant is the warm, diffuse glow of candlelight from hanging hurricane lamps.

While Nick and Dalila wait for their meal, a storm from the east lingers momentarily over Charlotte Amalie and dumps a torrent of rain. Canvas awnings protect the restaurant's patrons from the downpour without obstructing the vista. The intoxicating effect of being awash in the storm's fresh air is followed by a caress from the trade winds pushing the squall west.

Nick refills their wine glasses with the generic Bordeaux that is the restaurant's only red offering.

"You think we have a chance?"

"No sweat. We're going to find the lab and stop this guy."

"You're very confident. Is that from experience?"

"There's no other endgame that's acceptable."

"So we do what we have to do?"

"Something like that, but there are limits."

"What are the limits?"

"Believe it or not, there are some things I just won't do. If not, I'm no different from Kropotkin."

"You're worlds apart. You needn't fret about it."

"I don't, for the most part."

"I'm spoiling our beautiful evening with questions that have no answers."

"Not at all. Ask me anything."

"My first question was really about the two of us."

"I'm a better field agent than analyst."

"And what are your field agent instincts telling you?"

"How do you like island life?"

"Life in the tropics? I love it. It's beautiful here. But I love Kenya, too. And I want to go back when we're done here."

"Do you miss it?"

"I haven't been homesick since I went off to London as a schoolgirl, if that's what you mean."

"No. Something deeper."

"I should miss its people if I didn't return. I love the people of Kenya, my people, and I want to be their servant, their heroine even."

"We're not so different."

"I've always been told opposites attract."

"Nonsense."

Nick reaches for her hand.

"Our little headquarters is getting crowded," Dalila whispers.

"I know a place nearby with a pool."

"A midnight swim?"

"I'll take you there after dinner."

Dalila leans in and whispers, "Take me now, Nick."

CHAPTER 61

LAB RAT

It is near midnight when Schnelling finishes the third and final review of his calculations. The figures confirm that the pace of production exceeds his expectations. He is two days ahead of schedule; four more days in the lab will do it rather than six. He'll soon have enough of the formula for the six two-liter cylinders, one for each target city. Allocating the formula to the containers, threading a valve welded to a suitable dip tube in each, sealing the valve and pressurizing the filled containers should take no more than three hours once production is complete.

Schnelling is aware that pressurizing the cylinders before he removes them from the lab increases the risk of an inadvertent release en route. He has to balance that possibility against potential incompetence at the cell level stateside. He knows nothing about the capabilities of the five men and one woman responsible for the final stage of the mission, a reasonable security precaution. With that in mind, he decided to nearly eliminate the need for any sort of technical expertise at the point of delivery.

The plan calls for each cell member to simply place a single pressurized cylinder in a crowded public space, open its valve, and walk briskly up wind and away from the cylinder's crippling emission. Any traitor worth his salt should be able to handle it. The odorless formula, having no immediate effects, will cause no concern if it is noticed at all. Its devastation will become apparent days and weeks later, at which time it will be too late. It is the perfect weapon: cheap, almost undetectable, and brutally destructive, both physically and psychologically.

He turns the light out as he leaves the main production room. The flames of three small gas burners needed in the process will provide the only remaining light until he returns to conduct a routine and detailed inspection of the lab's functioning equipment four hours hence. He walks past the small radio room where he'll forward instructions for the early extraction during tomorrow's scheduled transmission. He passes through a set of swinging metal doors into the small living quarters that will be his home for his last days on St. Thomas. He checks a panel of lights above his personal desk. Four red lights indicate a reasonably secure, booby-trapped perimeter. A fifth light tells him the generator is functioning as designed.

Schnelling sits on his cot, checks his watch, and winds and sets his small travel alarm clock to go off at 4:00 a.m. He removes his glasses, sets them on his desk and, without undressing, stretches out on his cot and thinks about the approaching climax of more than two years of work.

Four more days and he'll be off the island, away from the meddling Americans; four more days and the personal fortune waiting for him in a Swiss bank account will be one step closer to being his; four more days and his dream of engineering a strike as psychologically devastating as any in the history of warfare will be one step closer to being a reality. Four more days.

CHAPTER 62

UNDER SAN CRISTOBAL'S MOON

Since their small, canvas, two-man shelters are too stifling for sleep, Dmitri Bogdonevitch and Yuri Belyavski lie on cots in the open air near Cuba's recently constructed San Cristobal missile launch site. At a little past two in the morning Dmitri reaches for his shirt on the folding camp table next to his cot. Using only the light of the moon, he finds his cigarettes and matches in his shirt pocket. He pulls a cigarette out of the pack, lights it, and returns both items to his shirt pocket. He returns his shirt to the table, lies back on his cot, and smokes.

Moments later his lifelong friend speaks up.

"Smoking in bed in dangerous, Dmitri."

"You mean to tell me that what I'm doing might cause my sudden, violent death?"

"If you wish to put it that way."

"Smoking in bed is not so different from putting missiles in Cuba."

"Your counterrevolutionary attitudes are troubling."

"I'm not a counterrevolutionary. I'm a realist."

"You're a defeatist, which I'm told is just as bad as a counterrevolutionary, although I'm not entirely clear on the distinction."

"Then tell me, Yuri, what do you suppose is going to happen over the next few days?"

"We'll finish our work and then return home as heroes."

"You listen too closely at those awful political meetings."

"Another defeatist attitude. How will you learn without listening?"

"I listen, but what I listen to tells me more than I'll learn at any political meeting."

"What do you listen to?"

"Lately, I've been listening to the sounds of our own work. These sounds tell me the end is near."

"Another defeatist attitude. That's three by my count. You should stop talking so much, especially when you should be sleeping. Besides, when you talk I can't sleep."

"I don't want to waste my last days on earth sleeping."

"A clearly counterrevolutionary statement, I think. I'll have to report you to the Zampolit."

"Go ahead. Perhaps they'll ship me to Siberia before the shooting starts. It may be my only chance."

"You think the Americans will fire on us?"

"Why would they not?"

"Perhaps you should give me a cigarette."

"Is it no longer dangerous to smoke in bed?"

"One end is as good as the next, I suppose."

"Now it is you who utters defeatist propaganda."

"Then with luck we'll both be sent to Siberia before the Americans start a war."

Dmitri fishes another cigarette out of his pack, hands it to Yuri and tosses the pack of matches to him.

"Strange what passes for luck these days."

CHAPTER 63

OCTOBER CHILL

The apartment of Yevgeny and Zenaida Kasparanov is buttoned up against a cold October dawn. Cigarette smoke and steam from a boiling tea kettle make the cramped apartment seem even smaller. The first hints of a long Moscow winter are greeted with resigned familiarity by the young couple.

"Yevgeny, the kitchen window still leaks. Maybe we can get it fixed this year?"

"I like to think of it as our only source of fresh air for the next six months."

"What?"

"That way I don't see it as broken."

"You need a vacation. When do you get a vacation?"

"When I lose my job."

"I just realized this morning that it's been more than a year since we spent any time out of Moscow."

"There are worse places, believe me."

"What good is it being a big shot in the government if you have to work like a dog?"

"I'm not a big shot yet."

"When?"

"The next few days are critical. Either I'll be the big shot you dream about, or . . . or I don't know what I'll be."

They sit silently smoking, sipping their tea until they hear their daughter call.

"Mama!"

Their mood changes instantly, both of them delighted to hear Tatyana's sweet musical voice.

"Tatyana's up. Go get her out of bed. She doesn't get to see her father enough."

Yevgeny puts out his cigarette and heads for the apartment's lone bedroom. His daughter, sitting on her bed, squeals with delight when she sees him.

"Papa! Pick me up! Pick me up!"

Yevgeny Kasparanov, who like most fathers cannot resist the commands of this beautiful three-year-old, bends down, picks her up, and hugs her tightly.

"Shall we go see Mama?"

Tatyana looks at her father and simply nods before she hugs him tightly around the neck again.

Yevgeny, nearly in tears, carries his daughter to the kitchen.

"We are ready for our breakfast," he announces.

"I'll help Mama!"

Yevgeny puts his daughter down. She runs to her mother and hugs her, wrapping her arms around her mother's legs.

The phone in the living area rings. Zenaida looks impatiently at Yevgeny. He goes to answer it.

"Yes. . . Yes, of course. I'm about to finish my breakfast and I'll be there as soon as I'm done. . . Yes, please let him know. Thank you."

He returns to the kitchen and sits at the table.

"Shouldn't you go?"

"Soon. First, I want to spend some time with my two favorite girls."

Zenaida walks up behind him and kisses him on top of his head.

"I'll get breakfast started for the three of us. You can think about the rest of the world later."

CHAPTER 64

TWO MAPS, ONE PLAN

The veranda table is covered with two sets of maps. The first set contains the USGS maps covering the north shore of St. Thomas; the second includes the nautical maps for the same areas. Team Temple inspects the maps to prioritize their search for Schnelling's lab. The earlier attempt to simply spot the lab from the water proved inadequate, so this morning has been all about the analytical work to focus their pending search. That work has resulted in the identification of nine north shore locations that appear suitable for both a land-based operation and safe, open-water access, from Tutu Bay, just west of the channel between St. Thomas and Thatch Cay, to Sandy and Botany Bays near the western tip of the island.

"Schnelling gets there in a Volvo, so there has to be a serviceable road to the lab, even if it's not much more than a trail. We'll split up. I'll take Dalila and Cristobal out from Frenchtown on another charter. Kyle, you Pete and Raoul will work the roads along the coastline. If you find his lab, don't approach it unless you're sure it's deserted. Watch out for trip wires. We know that's Schnelling's style. If it's clear, Pete, you'll need to head in, take a look, and tell us what you can about where he is in the process, what he's accomplished so far, and how much longer you think he'll need until he's finished with whatever he's started. Or, worst case scenario, if he's done. Frankly, if he's not there, then he's probably done with the lab work and off the island."

"Looking forward to it," is Pete's reply.

"We'll keep abreast of each other by radio and work one bay at a time until we either find something or we're satisfied there's nothing there. We should have enough daylight to thoroughly recon three locations each day."

Nick checks his watch.

"We're signing out the charter in about 30 minutes. It should have three days' provisions on it. Since we've already lost some daylight, we'll start on the west side of the island: Sandy Bay and Botany Bay first, then on to Stumpy Bay. After finishing at Stumpy Bay, we'll anchor off Santa Maria Bay for the night and start working our way east again first thing in the morning. There are two berths in the cabin of the Constellation; we'll each take a three-hour watch overnight.

"Kyle, the way the roads look, you should be able to get close to Sandy Bay in well under an hour. We'll stay in contact, but don't wait for us. Probe the coast and the trails west of Fortuna Road. If you see a passable trail, check it out. We have to make sure we cover every possible way in. We can't miss this time around. Questions?"

Nick looks around at the group. When no one speaks up, Nick resumes.

"Okay. Let's load up. Cristobal, grab the nautical maps. We've got the Jeep. We'll do a comms check on the two angry fives as soon as we're under way. They're bulky but rugged and dependable. I don't want to get caught with our pants down if the charter's radio goes out. We'll keep the comms simple but we still need to rotate frequencies and call signs per SOP. Kyle can fill you in. Firepower's in the trunk in my room. No telling what we might be up against. We'll take the M14s on the boat.

Clips are loaded. Kyle, you and Raoul make sure you've got plenty of ammo for both Raoul's .45 and your Beretta. Sidearms only at this point for you."

"Got it."

The team members gather up the maps and quickly, resolutely prepare to execute a mission that may be the last best hope for millions of Americans.

CHAPTER 65

SHOPPING SPREE

The 36-foot Chris-Craft Constellation Nick chartered for the earlier shoreline search sits tied up once again in Frenchtown. Nick and the charter company's representative are engaged in an unexpected round of negotiations as Cristobal and Dalila get the team's duffel bags out of the Jeep and onto the boat.

"That's bullshit. We had a deal. Three days at the hourly rate."

"There's nothing I can do about it. I have my orders."

"And I have mine. Are the provisions on board?"

"Well, yes."

"Then this is nothing more than a stick up."

"Depends on your point of view, I suppose."

"Point of view my ass. Wait here."

Nick returns to the Jeep. He pulls a pen and a small check register out of the glove compartment. He puts the register on the car's roof, writes a check, tears it out of the register and returns the register and pen to the glove compartment.

Nick walks back to the rep and hands him a check from the U.S. Treasury.

"What the hell is this?"

"I just bought your boat."

"It isn't for sale."

"You're right. Uncle Sam owns it and he's not selling it. Or would you prefer I requisition it with a promise to pay up later? We can go that route. Either way, the boat's mine. I'm just trying to be fair."

"What?"

"Look. I haven't got time for this. Take the check to Government House. They'll authenticate it for you. You've already got the cash for the three days. If the draft doesn't clear you can call the cops when three days are up, but I'm going to warn you that doing anything other than cashing that check, which is for a helluva lot more than your fucking boat's worth, would be a very bad idea. Got it?"

Nick leaves the stunned rep staring at the check.

"Everything set?" Cristobal asks.

"The cruise is a little more expensive than our earlier estimates."

"He squeeze you for more dough?"

"Lots more, but the boat's ours. Consider it the latest addition to the U.S. Navy. Let's get under way. Dalila, I'll get the lines; you get us out of here."

Dalila heads for the helm. Anyone seeing her dressed in white sneakers, navy blue Capri pants, and a light yellow sleeveless blouse could not be blamed for thinking she is simply a beautiful woman about to spend the day relaxing on a luxury yacht cruising the Caribbean. But her appearance belies her focus and dedication to the mission which, a focus that is every bit as intense as that of her teammates. Nick can't help thinking how perfectly suited she is to this work, and how lucky he is to have her on board.

She starts the Constellation's twin diesel engines. Cristobal takes the bow line from Nick and stows it on the forward deck in a Flemish coil. Nick releases the stern line from a cleat on the pier and jumps on board with the line in his hand.

"Okay, Dalila. Take us out."

Dalila engages the twin screws and, mindful to synchronize the RPMs for the two engines, opens the throttles and slowly guides the boat away from the pier and into the bay. The lessons Nick gave her on their first cruise stuck, and now she works the helm with confidence and skill.

CHAPTER 66

SHINY NEW OBJECT

Yevgeny Kasparanov's latest audience with the General Secretary comes amid unprecedented tensions between the Soviet Union and the United States. Military giants have flailed at each other for thousands of years, but never with the destructive potential of nuclear weapons. The sheer terror instilled by what appears to be the high probability of all-out nuclear war has brought the civilian world nearly to a halt as the cataclysmic standoff unfolds on the world stage.

"Your diversion is working as intended, Yevgeny Nikolaievitch. The reports confirm that every level of American government is consumed by what our heroic forces are accomplishing in Cuba. And we have no indication of additional assets being committed to stop your German professor. But it won't last forever. It can't last forever. In my view, he has less than a week. The Americans have a short attention span, and they will get back to work on other matters soon, even in the face of the threat from Cuba. What news do you have from the island?"

"He is secure in his lab for the final push. As planned, he is now communicating via radio with our modest gunboat. He reports that he is certain he'll be done on St. Thomas three days from today with immediate insertion and dispersal to follow within 72 hours of when he leaves the island."

"Three days. That's when I'll make the private overture. The timing is right. It's an enormous gamble, but I am certain that peering over the brink will restore some sanity to a process whose outcome has been merely theoretical to this point."

"For both nations?"

"What choice does either have? In this case mass murder, a viable tactic or strategy under the correct circumstances, is nothing more than collective suicide which can never be rationalized. Our gamble rests on the assumption that the aspirations and fears of both sides are still subject to a degree of rational decision making."

"Then there is nothing more for me to do other than wait."

"That is incorrect, my young friend. If you were thinking of spending some time at home, I am sorry to disappoint you. Your continued presence on the job signals confidence of success in both matters. Staying away would be interpreted as fear of failure. Except to go home for a few hours of sleep and a change of clothes, you should plan on being in your office for the duration."

Yevgeny stands to leave.

"Then I'd better get to my post. I'll keep you informed of Schnelling's progress."

"Of course."

As Kasparanov is leaving the General Secretary's office, the intercom on his desk buzzes. He flips a switch and responds.

"Yes?"

"The Americans have issued a statement."

"Bring it to me."

It will be up to the General Secretary, irrespective of the rhetoric the Americans employ, regardless of the predictable demands they make, to propose a way out of the deadly labyrinth he and his countrymen have created. It will be up to the Americans, irrespective of forces within their own government and those around the world, to interpret and respond to his proposal sanely and rationally. While the prospect of failure is unthinkable, the General Secretary of the Communist Party of the Soviet Union fears in his heart that the chances of failure are great.

CHAPTER 67

HUNTING REDS IN OCTOBER

"Roger. Nothing to report. We'll anchor here for the night. Ready to go at zero six hundred hours. Over."

"Roger. Out."

Nick switches off the radio.

"They're heading back for the night. That's it for today. Three bays down, six to go, and no sign of Schnelling. We'll scour Santa Maria in the morning. Let's set the anchor."

With the last traces of twilight fading quickly, Cristobal Guzman heads forward on the 36-foot Chris-Craft Constellation to lower its anchor. According to their charts, they are in just under five fathoms of water. Nick waits at the helm for Cristobal's signal.

"It's on the seabed, Nick."

Nick slowly backs the boat as Cristobal allows the anchor rode to pay out. After the anchor grabs on the seabed Cristobal continues to pay out the half-inch rode until he deploys 60 meters of it.

"That'll do it, Nick."

Nick kills the twin engines. Cristobal ties off the rode by securing it to the bow cleat and returns aft along the boat's port sidedeck to the helm.

"No anchor light?" Cristobal asks Nick.

"We're going to have to take our chances."

"I'll take the first watch," he tells Nick.

"Good."

Nick checks his watch.

"Three hours each. That should get us to dawn. I'll be your relief."

Nick turns to Dalila.

"We should get below and try to get some sleep."

Cristobal hops down from the sidedeck to the wheelhouse while Dalila leads Nick down the companionway. The forward cabin has two bunks on the starboard side with a small galley to port.

"Top or bottom bunk?"

"I prefer to be on top."

"I know. Top or bottom bunk?"

Dalila sizes up the two bunks.

"Too small to share?"

"Our friend is within earshot."

"I wouldn't want to embarrass anybody."

Nick pulls her to him and they share a long, luxurious kiss.

"I'll take the bottom bunk. Less chance of disturbing you when I go on watch."

"After that kiss, I doubt I'll be able to sleep, Mr. Temple," Dalila whispers.

"That makes two of us, Miss Atieno. Good night."

They kiss once more, taking their minds for a brief moment away from the dangers lying just over the horizon.

Before calling it a night, Schnelling scans the waters of Santa Maria Bay once more through his binoculars. A boat! At the northwest end of the bay! Its silhouette on the horizon is barely visible against the night sky. Schnelling's focus is intense, but due to the late hour he cannot discern any details beyond the craft's profile. It must be the Americans; it's too much of a coincidence. In almost two years he has never seen a boat anchor overnight in the bay. He looks again. The boat has not changed position. They've anchored. But for how long? When did they arrive?

He sets the binoculars down and tries to compose himself. Should he radio for assistance? Should he have himself and the three canisters that are ready for deployment transferred off the island immediately? Should he ignore the boat, hoping they will once again be unable to detect the lab's presence?

His options are limited and each is fraught with its own hazards. If the Americans detect his presence and he has no assistance, they will have a clear firepower advantage. All will be for naught; all will be lost. If they don't spot him and he calls for assistance, he'll reveal his position, and there's no guarantee that they have just the one boat. Do the Americans have additional resources closing in on him from the east or overland from the south side of the island? Doing nothing is the option with the biggest reward: non-detection, and the biggest risk: termination before transport. Schnelling decides the risk is too great. Three cylinders will have to do. A fourth may be ready in time.

He heads for the R-104M in the lab's small radio room, grabs the code book stuffed under the leather strap on the top of the radio, and begins to compose his request for immediate removal and whatever firepower is available. The extraction team sitting in Gustavia, St. Barts is already on high alert and should be able to make Santa Maria Bay sometime tomorrow morning. With no other acceptable options open to him, Schnelling turns on the radio to begin his transmission.

CHAPTER 68

TWO BY SEA

"You should have at least tried to sleep."

Nick continues to scan the bay as he responds.

"And miss three hours alone with you anchored off a tropical island? It was that or a couple of hours of tossing and turning in a stuffy cabin with Cristobal snoring away. Easy choice."

Cristobal comes up from the companionway and joins Nick and Dalila on the aft deck.

"I stopped snoring and made some coffee."

Nick laughs, lets the binoculars hang from his neck, and pats his friend on the back.

"You weren't supposed to hear that."

"You and my wife should compare notes."

"I'll pass."

"Even my kids give me a hard time about snoring."

"How many kids?"

"Two girls. Third one's on the way. My wife wants a boy, but I like daughters. Either way, we've agreed three's enough."

"What's your wife's name?" Dalila asks.

"Edelma. Mugs are hanging in the galley."

"That's a beautiful name. Thank you, Cristobal. Nick, would you like a cup?"

"Absolutely."

"How do you take it?"

"Black."

Dalila heads for the galley.

"Any action?"

"Nothing all night."

Nick checks his watch.

"Kyle should be coming up on the radio in five minutes. We'll get back to work as soon as we hear from him."

A flash of reflective light from the tree line just past the bay's white sand beach catches Cristobal's eye.

"Give me the glasses."

Nick takes the binoculars off his neck and hands them to Cristobal.

"What'd you see?"

"A flash, like something reflecting the sun. About 20 meters in from the beach, towards the east end of the bay. There it is again. Same spot."

Hartmut Schnelling finishes opening the three small windows on the north side of his living quarters. Each opens up and out from the bottom to let some of the cooler morning air in. When he finishes opening the third, he notices the silhouette of the boat against the northern sky. It has not moved since last night. He picks up his binoculars. The early morning sun provides enough light to make out some details from his position. He sees two men standing along the boat's aft starboard rail looking directly at his location through their binoculars. He sees one of the men, the younger of the two, point in the lab's direction. The older man, the meddlesome American he has been trying to eliminate for months, seems to give the younger man some instructions. The younger man takes two steps away from rail and towards the wheelhouse on the port side. He picks up the mic of a radio and begins to talk into it. They both point as he talks. There is no doubt in Schnelling's mind; his position is compromised! Where is the boat from St. Barts?

Four full, pressurized canisters stand ready for immediate crating and shipment. Two more will be ready within 24 hours. The boat from Gustavia is his only chance. But where is it?

←—↔→↔→↔→↔→↔→↔—→

Raoul sits in the passenger seat of the Rambler. Kyle Richardson drives, and Pete Hall shares the backseat with the team's radio. Raoul focuses on the map in his lap as they bounce along St. Thomas's primitive roads.

"Okay, we'll check out the visual Nick and Cristobal picked up. We can get within about 150 meters of Santa Maria Bay on this switchback trail off of Fortuna Road. We'll take it east and west and look for spurs north to the water. Kyle, bear left at the fork onto Fortuna. We should be at the bay in less than 15 minutes. Take the fork to the left at West End Road."

Raoul turns to Pete in the back seat.

"Pete, let's break out the hardware. Small bag."

Pete Hall hands the small canvas bag on the seat next to him to Raoul.

"Just sidearms should do it. You ever fire one of these?" Raoul asks Pete as he pulls one of the three .45 caliber M1911s out of the bag.

"I used to hunt for frogs on my grandfather's farm with a .22, a rifle, but that's about it."

"Frogs? With a rifle? This is easier. And the prey is bigger, easier to hit."

After explaining the weapon's grip safety, Raoul proceeds to show Pete how to insert a seven-round magazine, load the first round into the chamber, operate the thumb safety, and eject the magazine once it's empty.

"Once the first round is in the chamber and the safety's off, just point and shoot. Nice and simple. Hopefully, it won't come to that, but Nick said he doesn't want anyone running around in the bush unarmed, and that includes you. Here. Safety's on."

He hands the loaded semi-automatic pistol to Pete.

"Like you said, I hope it doesn't come to that."

Cristobal spots the boat just as he's weighing and securing the anchor. A small, fast boat, heading straight for them from the east. If it maintains its course and speed, it'll be within small arms range in less than two minutes.

"Looks like the cavalry's here!" he shouts as he scrambles aft.

The approaching boat is faster and more maneuverable than the Chris-Craft. Nick knows there's no sense in running, but sitting still would be suicide. Cristobal reaches the aft deck and looks to Nick at the helm for instructions.

"Get on the horn to Raoul. We need some onshore fireworks ASAP," Nick commands as he opens the throttle on both engines and cuts the wheel hard to port. "I'll run north by northwest to increase their closing time."

Cristobal races to the radio, picks up the mic, dials the morning's frequency, and begins to transmit.

"Ramblin' Man, this is Surf Rider. Come in, over."

"Dalila, we need some firepower on deck," Nick shouts over his shoulder.

Dalila heads below to the stash of light weapons they brought on board in Frenchtown.

Cristobal repeats the call, releases the push-to-talk button on the mic and waits. The radio crackles with Raoul's response.

"Surf Rider, this is Ramblin' Man. Over."

"Ramblin' Man, we've got a boat closing fast from the east. What's your location?

"Approximately one hundred meters south of the beach."

"Okay. We need some fireworks on the beach. Light it up. We'll see if he takes the bait."

"Roger, Surf Rider. Out."

"Stop here."

Kyle immediately pulls the Rambler to the side of the trail and stops.

"Keep the engine running."

Raoul gets out, pops open the Rambler's trunk, and unzips a large sea bag of weapons and explosives. He retrieves an M8 40mm flare gun and four signal cartridges. He loads a cartridge through the flare gun's open breech, closes the breech, steps into the middle of the trail, and fires the flare between the overhead trees in the direction of Santa Maria Bay. He repeats the action three more times before returning to the car's open trunk. He grabs a small wooden box of six M26 fragmentation grenades, slams the trunk close, jumps in the car, and shuts the door behind him.

"We've got to get to the beach, just behind the tree line."

"I'll see what I can do."

Kyle puts the Rambler in gear and moves east along the trail. After travelling less than 50 meters he spots an opening in the dense vegetation lining the trail. He looks at Raoul.

"It's worth a shot," Raoul suggests.

Kyle cuts the wheel to the left and soon the Rambler is bouncing along what is little more than a wide footpath. Another 30 seconds and they can see the beach beyond a tree line ten meters ahead.

"Here's good. Kyle, you've got the sidearms and clips."

Kyle stops the car. Pete hands Kyle the bag of M1911s and fully-loaded clips. The men jump out of the car.

Raoul rips the top off the box of grenades, pulls out two grenades, hands one each to Pete and Kyle, and grabs two for himself.

"Follow me," he commands.

Raoul heads for the beach and stops among a group of flamboyant, bottlebrush, and palm trees just short of the open sand. They see the Chris-Craft racing for the open water. The other boat has momentarily broken off the chase and is circling slowly. A crew member near its transom is searching the sky.

"Looks like the flares got his attention," Kyle notes.

Raoul turns to Pete who nervously clutches his grenade.

"It's simple, Pete. Hold the grenade so the clip won't pop when you pull the pin; slip your finger through the ring; pull hard on the pin; toss the grenade and take cover. They're five-second fuses. Close your eyes and cover your ears. The concussion from three grenades will be brutal. We'll do all three at once, straight out towards the water. I'll pitch the fourth one as soon as the dust settles. That should give Nick time to decide his next move. Pick a tree for cover."

The three men spread out.

"Ready?"

Kyle and Pete nod.

"Pull the clip on three and let it fly. One, two, three!"

The men pull the clips, throw the grenades towards the beach's high tide mark, and take cover. Two of the grenades hit the gentle surf while the third lands just shy of the water. The tremendous blast created by the three grenades detonating nearly simultaneously sends fragments, sand, water and a few species of aquatic life flying. Before sand and smoke have cleared Raoul stands up and pulls the clip on the fourth grenade.

"Stay down!"

He tosses the grenade a little farther east on the beach than the others. Again, five seconds after the pin is pulled the effect is intense. The blast sends all manner of debris, together with the deadly fragments from the grenade shooting off into an empty kill zone.

Raoul checks on the other men.

"Everyone all right?"

He gets a thumbs-up from Pete and Kyle.

"Let's hope that did the trick."

The boat from Gustavia has halted its pursuit of the Chris-Craft and is idling in the shallow end of the bay, no more than 100 meters west of the three men. From their position, Raoul and the others can see a tripod-mounted, 7.62mm Soviet PK machine gun near the boat's transom. A crew member in civilian clothes stands at the machine gun, pointing it in the general direction of Nick's boat, ready to fire.

Hartmut Schnelling is sweating profusely as he taps the last six-penny nail into the small shipping crate containing the first of the four pressurized containers. The American boat, the boat from Gustavia, and the flares all sent him into a frenzy of activity. Just as he finishes closing the crate's lid with one last throw of his hammer, he hears the grenades explode! Three go off at once followed closely by a fourth.

Desperate to begin the transport of the canisters, he picks up the crate and heads out of the lab towards the beach.

Dalila keeps an eye on the other boat.

"Nick, they're anchoring almost on shore. If they're not careful, they'll run aground."

"Thanks, Dalila. Cristobal, take the wheel and head us straight for them. Let's take our best shot at them with the M14s. They're our only chance against that PK they've got mounted in their stern."

Cristobal takes the wheel.

"Hold on!"

With the boat reaching top speed, he cuts the wheel hard to starboard. The Chris-Craft executes a long 180-degree turn. Cristobal brings the wheel back around and steers a course directly for the boat now anchored just off the beach of Santa Maria Bay.

←—←→←→←→←→←→—→

Kyle is the first to see him.

"That's our professor. What the hell is he carrying?"

No more than fifty meters down the beach, Schnelling carries the crate containing a canister of deadly, pressurized formula straight for the anchored boat. A crew member waits in a foot of water to retrieve the crate from Schnelling.

Kyle takes control.

"Hold your fire. If that crate is what I think it is, we can't risk hitting it. Wait until he's handed it over."

Schnelling hands the crate to the crew member who wades slowly back to the anchored boat with the crate held high over his head. Schnelling turns to head back to his lab.

"That's it. We can't let him transfer another one of those damn things. Open fire!" Kyle shouts.

The three men pour a fusillade of small arms fire towards Schnelling. One round hits him in the upper thigh of his right leg, dropping him to the beach.

"Cease fire and take cover!" Kyle orders.

The three men run for the cover of the dense bush back from the beach. They hit the ground as the gunner on the back of the boat pins them down by spraying 7.62mm rounds in their direction. Bullets rip through the foliage directly above them, but none finds its mark. After about ten seconds, the firing stops.

The crew member carrying the crate over his head, in water up to his chest, hands the crate to the gunner and boards the boat by climbing a small rope ladder.

Kyle uses the break in the firing to low crawl back towards the beach. He stops just shy of the beach, stands up next to a palm tree, takes careful aim with his .45, and puts a bullet in the temple of the crawling, bleeding Professor Hartmut Schnelling. The response from the gunner is immediate and furious. With rounds crashing through the air all around him, Kyle drops, rolls, and then low crawls desperately through the dense undergrowth back to the position of Raoul and Pete. He reaches his companions miraculously unscathed.

With Schnelling dead on the beach and the Chris-Craft bearing down on them, the crew of the boat from Gustavia quickly weighs anchor, throws the engine into reverse, and backs away from the beach for deeper water. The gunner wheels the PK around and fires five-round bursts at the approaching Chris-Craft. Their destination is a refueling stop in the Turks and Caicos.

"They're pulling out! Pour it on!"

Nick and Dalila continue to fire their M14s at the enemy craft. The return fire from the mounted PK machine gun is furious.

"Open it up. Everything you've got, Cristobal!"

Cristobal Guzman complies, pushing the engines to their limits as Nick and Dalila fire at will.

The small, seemingly harmless sound of a round cracking the glass of the wheelhouse causes Nick to turn. He sees Cristobal grab his throat with both hands and stagger back from the wheel. Blood pours through his fingers before he collapses on the aft deck.

"Get down!" Nick shouts to Dalila. She kneels behind the gunwale but keeps firing her M14. Nick runs to the boat's wheel, undoes his belt buckle and removes his belt in a split second. He uses his belt to secure the wheel to the throttle of the starboard engine so the boat roughly maintains its course. He turns to Cristobal who is lying face up on the deck, still clutching his profusely bleeding throat.

With rounds ripping through the superstructure of the wheelhouse, Nick grabs a first aid kit from the netting on the ceiling, rips it open, and pulls out a large compression bandage and a roll of gauze to stop Cristobal's bleeding. Nick kneels down by his struggling comrade and pulls his hands from his throat. The size and severity of the wound are shocking. Although Nick knows Cristobal has less than 30 seconds to live, he places the compression bandage directly on the wound and secures it by quickly wrapping the gauze around the dying man's neck. There's nothing else to do except wait. He cradles Cristobal's head in his lap.

"Don't worry, buddy. We'll get you home. We'll see that you get home."

Cristobal's bloody hand searches for Nick's. Nick grabs it a moment before all of the strength goes out of it.

Cristobal Guzman, father of two with one on the way, is dead.

Dalila turns to see Nick still cradling Cristobal's head and holding his hand. She puts down her M14 and scrambles to the boat's helm. She undoes Nick's belt, reduces the RPMs of both engines to barely more than idling, and cuts the wheel to starboard.

"They're out of range. We lost them."

Nick looks up at her.

"Cristobal's dead."

Dalila, suppressing a sob, goes to Nick and kneels beside him with her hand on his back.

"We need to get him ashore, Nick."

Nick lets go of Cristobal's limp hand, sets his head gently on the deck, and stands up. He picks up a pair of binoculars sitting in netting slung under the gunwale, scans the beach, and sees Schnelling's body.

"War's been over for 17 years, and we're still killing Nazis. Good fucking riddance."

He continues scanning until he sees Kyle Richardson emerge from the tree line. Richardson signals for Nick to bring the Chris-Craft into the shallow end of the bay.

"Take us in, Dalila."

Dalila goes to the helm, increases the boat's speed, and steers a course for the beautiful and deadly bay of Santa Maria.

CHAPTER 69

THE ONE THAT GOT AWAY

Nick and Dalila, both wet from wading in, stand with Raoul just beyond the water's edge. The Chris-Craft is anchored ten meters out in waist-deep water. Kyle and Pete wait near the tree line.

"Make sure he gets home, Raoul."

"I'll wire the unit from Government House. They'll contact his wife."

"Do you know her?"

"Since he joined the force. She's pregnant. It's going to hit her hard."

"I'll call Langley. They'll take care of her."

"Thanks, Nick. I should go."

"Take the boat back to Red Hook. Find a slip and pay for a month in advance. We'll figure out what to do with it now that it belongs to Uncle Sam. Radio Government House before you get in so the coroner's waiting. Tell them no press. Nothing public."

"Of course."

"Jesus. It's an awful business we're in."

"He knew the risks."

Nick and Raoul shake hands. Dalila gives Raoul a hug before he wades out into the warm Atlantic towards the anchored boat carrying his dead friend. He climbs the aft swim ladder, heads to the helm without looking down at Cristobal's covered body, and starts the boat's twin engines. He eases the boat over the anchor, walks forward to pull it from the sandy bottom, and returns to the wheel. He points the bow towards the bay's entrance, opens the throttles, and speeds away.

Nick and Dalila shield their eyes against the morning sun as they watch Raoul motor out of sight.

"We've got work to do."

With that they turn and head to Kyle, Pete, and the lab of the late Professor Schnelling.

"A trip wire. No surprise."

Nick squats down to inspect the wire strung across the barely visible entrance to the lab. He follows the wire to a camouflaged detonator stuck into a package of C4 one foot above the ground. Anyone making contact with the wire would have both of his legs blown off from the knees down. Nick pulls the small detonator from the plastic explosive disarming the trap.

"I'm guessing there are more of these, so let's be alert. We don't need any more casualties."

Nick enters the building that contains Schnelling's living quarters and lab/production facility. Dalila and Pete are right behind him. All three, if asked, would have to admit they are impressed by their deceased adversary's ability to construct and hide for more than two years such a sophisticated, self-contained, and relatively extensive operation. It wasn't until they were practically on top of it that they recognized it for what it was. Its construction takes full advantage of the sugar plantation ruins and the surrounding vegetation to be undetectable from the air and nearly so from the ground. Their begrudging admiration quickly gives way to the task at hand.

"What exactly are we looking for?" Dalila asks.

"Pete, I want you to see what you can figure out about the science Schnelling was employing. Is there a cure? An antidote? Someway to neutralize the effects of the strain after exposure? Whatever you can determine about what he was doing that might help us defend against it both before and after release. Kyle's on the radio asking for help intercepting the boat, but we've already been told all assets operating in this theater are committed to the crisis in Cuba. We're probably still on our own."

"What about me?"

"You and I are going to look for a transmission log, a code book, instructions, drawings, maps, anything that might point us to where that container's going. Is it heading for one target? More than one target? What's the plan for dispersal? Airborne? Water system? Look for schematics, sequenced letters, lists of numbers that might give us a clue as to encryption. We don't have much time. That crate is on its way to the States, and we don't even know where they expect to make landfall."

Pete Hall wanders into Schnelling's lab. His first impression is that this is the workspace of a careful and meticulous professional. The area is small, free of clutter, well-organized, and efficiently laid out. This guy just happened to be a sick bastard to boot.

A long, sturdy, wooden table occupies the center of the room. On the table is a complex series of interconnected glass tubing and flow cocks through which a clear liquid from a large, air-tight, glass jar, suspended from the ceiling is being introduced. That liquid is augmented by the addition of other liquids from marked beakers sitting on stands over small gas burners at various points along the tubing, like tributaries feeding a larger stream. The beakers have black rubber stoppers with more glass tubing running from the bottom of each beaker through the stoppers and eventually connecting to the main section of the glass array.

"The production line," Pete thinks to himself.

Glass cabinets along the far wall contain two rows of clearly marked beakers with black rubber stoppers. Pete's experience tells him that each beaker contains an experimental sample. Another row contains active petri dishes each with spores in various stages of growth. They too are marked in grease pencil with a code that appears to connect them either to the rows of beakers in the cabinets or the beakers feeding the complex of glass tubing. The remaining cabinet space is taken up with microscopes, scales, burners, racks of test tubes, and just about any other piece of equipment a well-stocked lab might need.

A tall green tank of pressurized oxygen sits in the lab's far corner. The gauge on top of the tank's butterfly valve indicates it's less than half full. A clamped hose runs from the valve to a manifold near the end of the wooden table that can accommodate two canisters at a time. The manifold is designed to inject the liquid under production and then pressurized oxygen into the canisters. Clearly Schnelling contemplated pressurizing containers for the dispersal of his formula.

In addition to the two canisters at the manifold, three more sit near the lab's entrance. Pete inspects the gauges on those three tanks and satisfies himself that they are full and pressurized. The thought of what is in those tanks fascinates him professionally, and terrifies him personally.

Along the wall opposite the glass cabinets is a workbench with a number of bound volumes on a metallic shelf over the bench. These volumes become the focus of Pete Hall's attention as Nick and Dalila rummage through the rest of the premises. He sits on the high metal stool at the workbench and begins to go through the books.

"Beats firing pistols and throwing grenades," Pete thinks to himself.

Nick and Dalila have just located Schnelling's code book and log at the desk of his small living quarters when Pete Hall comes bursting in.

"It's all here, Nick, and it's all in the clear. Nothing's encrypted."

Pete Hall holds a thick, leather-bound volume he pulled from above the workbench.

"What have you got?"

"Production schedules – a total of six two-liter cylinders; delivery system – airborne dispersal; formula stability – it starts to deteriorate after a little under five days; and the final formula itself, including formulas for all unsuccessful attempts. And a lot more. Everything in fact. It's all here. It's in German, but I can read it. Part of the Ph.D. requirement."

"How many canisters are still in the lab?"

"Five."

"So the crate we saw being transferred to the boat is the only one that made it out of the lab?"

"I'm sure of it."

"That helps. Big time. We know we're just chasing the one. We find it, and that's the end of it."

"I didn't see anything in the lab about post-production activity. His journals are all about the science."

Nick shows him the code book he and Dalila found.

"That's probably in here. But it's not a code I'm familiar with. Christ, we don't have time to pore over this thing. We've got to break it and fast. We're playing catch up as it is."

Kyle joins them in the small quarters and reports in.

"St. Thomas Department of Public Safety is coming by for Schnelling. Hope they get him before the crabs do. Or not."

"Good. Any maritime help from our stateside friends?"

"Nada. All assets are dedicated. No change in the status quo."

"It was a long shot. Okay, Kyle, secure the lab. Disarm any additional booby traps you find. You might have to spend a couple of days here. It can't be helped. We can't leave this lab unguarded. Pete, you stay here and keep working. We need to come up with a safe plan for destroying Schnelling's work, and Langley's going to want those journals."

"You sure we shouldn't destroy those too?"

Pete's question is a good one, but Nick knows that the Company and Defense will be keenly interested in any weapons technology no matter how appalling its genesis or terrifying its effects.

"I'm sure we should destroy them, but that's not my call."

"Understood."

"Dalila and I'll take the car over to Government House right now. She'll bring the car back here after dropping me off. I'll see if I can't raise

Ted Durant or someone at NSA. The way I see it, we've probably got less than 24 hours to crack this code. It's our only chance. We know we're not going to get any help from the big boys on stopping that boat, if the canister's even still on board. The code's our only chance. I've got to make a call to Langley, too. Make sure Cristobal's family gets paid the debt our country owes them."

As Nick turns to leave he notices the three small open windows and looks out one of them.

"I bet the windows caught a bit of sun when he opened them this morning. It's a nice piece of luck that Cristobal was looking this way when Professor Nazi opened shop. Damn, that's a tough one to lose."

Nick and Dalila leave the building and walk to the parked Rambler. Pete and Kyle go back to the lab. The four of them know they are the only chance countless Americans have of escaping the cruelty of a sudden, crippling, and even fatal disease, the only chance those same Americans have of not becoming the latest victims in the clandestine struggles of the Cold War.

CHAPTER 70

THE RACE IS ON

"We're going to waste hours going through it over the phone. I need to see that log. How soon can you get to Miami?"

Ted Durant has been Nick's go-to guy on encryption for years. He's been using his Ph.D. in applied mathematics in service to his country since walking away from his comfortable life as a small college professor and enlisting on December 8, 1941. Ted's work was instrumental in unraveling what the Soviets were planning on Crete in '55. His intercept from a hotel room in Heraklion was a key piece in halting Moscow's ambitious and potentially game-changing gamble. If Ted Durant says it's a waste of time to try to crack Schnelling's code over the phone, that's good enough for Nick.

"I'll work on getting off the island as soon as I hang up."

"You know the USO lounge in the terminal at Miami International?"

"I do. I'll meet you there. I've got to make a call to Langley first."

"Guzman?"

"Yeah."

"Look, before you hang up, read whatever is written on the first and last pages of the log. It's a long shot, but I might be able to get started on the flight to Miami."

"Got it. Ready?"

"Shoot."

Nick reads the first page, a series of numbers and letters in groups of five that appear to repeat, but do not appear to be sentences; after finishing, he reads the last page which is again a combination of letters and numbers, in various-sized groups, arranged in a simple, horizontal, linear format the way sentences, with the notable absence of any punctuation, would normally appear in a western language.

"I want to read it back to you to make sure I've got it."

"Ready when you are."

Ted Durant and Nick Temple, World War II vets and long-time Cold War warriors, together do the tedious work, the far-less-than-glamorous work that so often is the difference between failure and success in their business.

As Durant and Temple work, a small, armed boat speeds towards a refueling stop on Parrot Cay off of North Caicos. From there it will make its way to a rendezvous with a practically anonymous commercial fishing boat in the Atlantic south of the Bahamas. Its deadly cargo is the one canister Schnelling managed to deliver is stored safely below; its destination is the sleepy South Carolina coastal town of Murrells Inlet where a panel van will be waiting. Target: Atlanta.

CHAPTER 71

ALPHABET SOUP

Nick Temple finds the waiting to be almost unbearable. He knows Ted Durant will ask for help if he wants it. Until then he's reduced to simply sitting in the small reception area of the USO lounge on the upper level of Miami International Airport's 20th Street Terminal.

Ted has been holed up in a small office behind the lounge since arriving three hours ago. Nick glances at his watch. It's nearly midnight. It's hard to believe that he started the day sharing a cup of coffee with Dalila at anchor off of Santa Maria Bay in St. Thomas. Nick is about to get up and ask the lone USO employee still working to make another pot of coffee when Ted comes bursting into the lounge.

"Nick. I think I've got him. He's good, but I think I have him."

"You think, or you know?"

"No. I know I've got him!"

"Let's have it."

Ted sits down in the faux leather armchair next to Nick. Schnelling's log is in one hand, and a legal pad, nearly every page covered with Durant's handwriting, and a pencil are in his other hand.

"I got thrown by what looked like the key on the first page, but he buried it. He was a smart guy. He stuck the key in at page 39. Smart as he was, he didn't trust his memory, so it's all in here: the key, the algorithm, the whole damn thing is all written down, starting at page 39. He probably relied on 1939 as a mnemonic device."

"That's great, Ted, and I don't mean to be a pain in the ass, but can we skip the crypto chalk talk and get down to what the log says?"

"Oh, yeah. Sorry. Of course. Six targets, all U.S. cities, all to be hit simultaneously."

"Got a date?"

"No. But neither did Schnelling. It's all tied to production. ASAP after production."

"What are the cities?"

"Okay. Let me see. I've got them cross-referenced. They're pretty early in the log. Looks like they settled on the targets fairly early in this process."

He puts the pencil behind his ear and flips the pages of his legal pad until he comes to a set of scribbled notes that only he can decipher. He then opens the code book to page 12.

"Here they are. Okay, he's got Atlanta, Chicago, Fresno, Moline, Portland, Maine, and St. Louis."

"Moline? Never heard of it."

"Illinois. Right on the Mississippi."

"Contacts?"

"Yeah. Each city. Each cell by name and address. The cells are all individuals. They're to take delivery, unload the canisters on a lunch-time crowd and get the hell out of the U.S. There are a variety of post-operation rendezvous points, a different one for each cell."

"So the sixty-four thousand dollar question is which city is the single canister going to?"

"Why not sit on all the contacts?"

"The country's already nearly in a panic. We'd need local law enforcement to do that, and in fairness we'd have to tell them what to expect so they'd be prepared. We do that and it's going to get out in a heartbeat. Throw that on top of nuclear missiles in Cuba and there's no telling what'll happen to the country, except that a full-scale panic would probably be the least of our worries with every nut job for 3,000 miles taking full advantage of the state of affairs. No, we've got to focus on and find that one canister that made it."

Ted shakes his head.

"I don't see anything in here to help us. His assumption was that all six would leave St. Thomas at once. So far as I can tell he had no contingency for any number less than that unless it's in another document."

"So we have no idea where it's headed? None? Come on, man. Do some of that analyst shit."

Ted doesn't respond for a moment. Suddenly his eyes light up and he snaps his fingers.

"Atlanta!"

"What?"

"Look, this guy is a detailed, meticulous guy. Typical scientist. No, typical *German* scientist. Everything is laid out, organized, and in some sort of perfect order. If we have to pick a target, I'd bet my paycheck that he had the targets in alphabetical order. My bet is Atlanta was first on his list."

"But you're not sure."

"No. But if you're not going to let us crash all six at once, if we have to pick one, then pick Atlanta. There's no logical reason, and no evidentiary basis for picking any of the other five."

Nick sits and thinks for a moment. Ted's right. Atlanta makes sense for Schnelling. But it's a gamble. They've come this far, and if they blow it now thousands of Americans, maybe tens of thousands of Americans are about to be poisoned and maimed, and the panic he's already worried about will surely follow. He doesn't see any alternative. Durant's as good as they come in this business, and sometimes it all comes down to trusting the best. Nick stands up.

"I'm going to Atlanta. You coming?"

"Damn right I am. Let's shut this asshole down."

CHAPTER 72

A BIRD IN HAND

"One canister? It can't be!"

Yevgeny Nikolaievitch Kasparanov stares at the decoded cable from Parrot Cay in disbelief. Schnelling is dead. The Americans have the lab and all of its contents, including presumably Schnelling's formula, and a single canister is headed to the American mainland. What was to be a widespread, psychologically and physically devastating attack designed to demonstrate the strategic, tactical, and technical superiority of the Soviet Union has been reduced to a single act of desperate and ugly terror. And there is no guarantee the Americans won't thwart the lone attack at this point. The entire operation is more likely than ever to be an unmitigated disaster.

He sits at his desk helpless, unable to render any assistance to make certain of the minimum success needed to salvage the operation, justify the expense, and save his own career or even his life. He thinks about calling his wife, but what would he tell her? Where can she and Tatyana go? There is no escape, and there is no one else to blame. He knows that his own ambition created this trap for the three of them.

The last canister is his only hope. If it makes it, he can claim he foresaw the odds as any field commander would and made certain enough assets were committed to ensure a level of success. Surely men who have witnessed the horrible slaughter of battle will appreciate such a point of view.

He checks the time stamp on the transmission one more time. He looks at his own watch and calculates the difference between the time zones. He should know within 12 hours if the single canister made it. The Atlanta cell, a lone patriot dedicated to the international cause, will surely report his success at the earliest possible moment. For now he can only sit and wait, hoping that the crisis in Cuba absorbs the full attention of the nation's military and political leaders.

The phone on his desk rings. He stares at it as it rings a second and third time. If for no other reason than to stop the phone's grating, maddening ringing, he picks up the receiver. Before he answers he tries to compose himself so that his voice, at least, does not betray his rising fear.

"Kasparanov here. . Yes, I've read it. . . Of course. . . By this time tomorrow. . .I'll remain available. . .Of course."

He hangs up, with the phrase "Make yourself available" ringing in his ears, a seemingly innocuous phrase that really means much more. He could have just as easily been told, "Don't make your arrest any more difficult than it has to be. There is no escape. Perhaps you should consider saving your family further humiliation by taking your own life."

The next 12 hours will decide his fate. With nothing left for him to do, he decides to spend the time at home with his small, vulnerable family. He stands up, grabs his light overcoat from the hook on the back of the door, turns out the light, and leaves his office for what may be the last time.

CHAPTER 73

A NEEDLE WITHOUT THE HAYSTACK

Alexei Boranov, known to his suburban Atlanta neighbors as Al Barone, has been on high alert since receiving the call from Murrells Inlet. He immediately left his home and, as prearranged, checked into a nondescript motel in Marietta, twenty miles to the north. Delivery is scheduled for 7 a.m., ten minutes from now.

His instructions are simple. Remove the canister from its crate, secure it to the bed of his pickup truck, leave the motel no earlier than immediately before checkout time of 11 a.m., drive to downtown Atlanta, set the canister on the sidewalk at noon, point the nozzle downwind, and open the valve releasing the deadly, airborne formula on the lunchtime crowd enjoying the sunshine and brilliant fall weather of Georgia's state capital.

Nick Temple and Ted Durant park in their rented Ford Galaxy 500 in front of Al Barone's two-bedroom, ranch style home on the east side of Atlanta. They get out, walk up the small sidewalk to the front door, knock, and wait.

"Nothing like the direct approach," Ted quips.

"I'm betting he's not here. My guess is he's taking delivery at a different loc. Let's see what we can find out."

Nick takes a quick look around. The commuters have left for work, the neighborhood kids are just starting school, and the quiet residential street is empty. He pulls a lock pick from his pocket and works the front doorknob. It gives way easily and they are quickly inside Al Barone's front room.

They begin to explore the house. The rooms are remarkably neat and free of any clutter. The two bedrooms' closets and chests of drawers are empty. The kitchen cabinets have plates, cups, glasses, and the usual utensils, but not a scrap of food. The refrigerator is empty. The two small bathrooms have brand new bars of soap on the sinks but are otherwise empty.

Nick and Ted finish their recon of the house and meet back in the living room.

"Weird. It's like a movie set, like no one actually lives here."

"This guy isn't coming back and didn't leave a clue."

"What's our next move?" Ted asks.

Nick thinks for a moment before responding.

"Let's check in with the Fulton County Sheriff. See if we can get a description, vehicle type, license plate number, anything that'll help us spot him. We're running out of time, and if you've got any better ideas, now's the time to share."

"I'm for checking in with the Sheriff."

The two men leave as they entered, through the front door. They hustle to their curbside car, get in, and speed away well aware at this point that time is on the side of their target.

Alexei Boranov checks his watch one more time. He is anxious yet resolute. He will follow the directives from Moscow to the letter. And now, at 10:55 a.m., on Friday, October 26th, he leaves his motel room with what anyone would mistake for a simple white propane canister in his hands, closes the door behind him, secures the canister in the bed of his pickup truck with two lengths of rope, and drives away, ready to strike a blow, to advance the glorious cause of worldwide Socialism!

The three men look at a detailed street map of downtown Atlanta spread out on the Sheriff's desk.

"If I wanted to scare the hell out of everybody, I'd put it right here, Washington Street, right in front of the capitol building, the heart of the government. A little breeze out of the west today. Not only does he get everyone coming out for lunch, but if he gets lucky he hits everyone still in that building. Its windows are going to be wide open on a day like today. Park your car half a block back down Washington to the west, set the damn thing on the sidewalk, open the valve, and walk away. Are you men sure about this? I'll be honest with y'all. It seems a little far-fetched."

Fulton County Sheriff Jim Morgan's first professional contact with the CIA is a whopper. If these two men are to be believed, then Atlanta is minutes away from a brutal attack. The quick confirmation from Langley of the identity of the men convinced him of their bona fides. The question now is how to stop this Boranov character before he completes his mission.

"We're sure. We just don't know where, but if what you say is true about that location, it's as good as any. Thanks, Sheriff. We'll take it from here."

"Look, Temple, there's going to be a helluva lot of people down there, which I suppose is the point. You can't just go firing up the place."

"Our plan is to take him down as soon as we see him, but we could use some help. Who's the best man on the force with a sidearm?"

"That's easy. Sam Coad. Wins the shootout at the qualification range every year."

"He's probably out in the field."

"Nope. Works a desk, believe it or not."

"Can we borrow him for about an hour?"

"He's all yours."

The Sheriff picks up his phone.

"Judy. Have Sam Coad come to my office ASAP."

He hangs up the phone.

"I think that's it. We've got his picture, his description-six feet two inches should work for us in a crowd-and a description of his vehicle. Mind if we take the file with us?"

"It's yours. You sure you don't want to muscle up?"

"I'm sure. We can't risk spooking him before we have a shot at securing that canister."

"Okay. It's your operation."

At that moment, there's a knock on the Sheriff's office door.

"That'll be Sam. Come in," the Sheriff commands.

Sam Coad–tall, lean, 25 years old, and a uniformed deputy–opens the door and pokes his head in.

"You wanted to see me, boss?"

"Sam, grab your sidearm and go with these men. They'll explain on the way. We're about to find out if you can shoot more than targets."

"Yes sir."

Nick sticks out his hand.

"Nick Temple. Nice to meet you. This is Ted Durant. We're both from D.C."

Nick and Sam shake hands.

"Let's get moving. We'll brief you in transit."

As the three men leave the Sheriff's office, Nick glances down at his watch: 11:37 a.m.

The traffic, heavy but moving, is typical for downtown Atlanta on a workday. Boranov looks at his watch as he waits in the right hand lane of Washington Street for the light to turn green. The capitol building is in view on his right. He crosses Trinity Avenue and looks for a parking spot. He pulls to the curb and parallel parks his truck.

Unnoticed by Boranov, a Galaxy 500 with three men in it, one a uniformed Sheriff's deputy, parks almost directly across Washington Street from him. All three men get out of the car and walk southwest to the corner of Washington and Trinity. They spot Boranov who is untying the canister secured in the bed of his pickup. Crowds of men and women emptying out of office buildings for lunch pass by him, oblivious to the danger.

Boranov removes the last length of rope and lifts the canister out of the truck. He slips into the crowd and walks on the sidewalk on the southeast side of Washington towards the Capitol. Nick, Ted, and Sam

Coad turn left at Washington after crossing. They are no more than 20 meters behind Boranov. They instinctively pick up the pace to close that gap.

"I'll take the first shot as soon as he sets the cylinder on the sidewalk. I'll go for a head shot above the crowd. If that doesn't stop him, you two finish him off. My shot should split the crowd. Aim center mass. We can't have rounds flying around all of these people."

Boranov stops at the corner of Mitchell Street and Washington. He walks to the side of the corner building.

"That's it. He's going to deploy," Nick says as he pulls his Beretta from his shoulder holster under his jacket.

Boranov sets the canister down. Nick fires off a round just as Boranov is bending down to open the valve. The round catches Boranov in the right shoulder. The crowd screams at the sound of gunfire. People scramble away from the wounded man. Some hit the pavement. Others stare in disbelief. Nick, Ted, and Sam, weapons drawn, stride towards their target.

Boranov reaches down for the valve with his left hand. Sam Coad fires a round that hits Boranov in his left hand. Boranov screams in pain, but he is undeterred. His right shoulder wound is not severe enough to disable his arm. He reaches for the canister valve with his remaining good hand. As Boranov's right hand touches the butterfly valve on top of the canister, Nick, Ted, and Sam pour a volley into his arms and upper body sending him sprawling past the canister to die on the sidewalk in front of the horrified crowd.

Nick can't tell if Boranov managed to open the valve to any extent. It has to be checked.

"Ted, wait here. Sam, see what you can do to calm this crowd down, but stay upwind of that canister," Nick orders.

Nick runs to the canister. Fully aware that he might be exposing himself to a high concentration of a disease that has haunted mankind for centuries, he bends down and torques the valve clockwise. It doesn't budge. He puts a finger at the valve's opening and feels nothing. Boranov never got it open. The canister sits inert, its deadly contents secure.

Nick motions to Ted who runs to assist him.

"Check on Boranov."

Ted walks over to the riddled body of Alexei Boranov. His eyes are wide open, but he is clearly dead. As Ted walks back to Nick and the canister, the first of many sirens begins to wail nearby. Nick looks up and can see police officers streaming out of the capitol, weapons drawn.

"Sam, we need your uniform over here now."

Sam Coad walks over to where Nick and Ted stand. Nick and Ted holster their weapons. Sam Coad addresses the approaching police officers.

"Sam Coad. Fulton County Deputy. Glad you fellas could join us. We've got some cleanup to do here. These men'll explain."

CHAPTER 74

THAT'S A WRAP

Their neighbors can't believe what they're seeing: solid, upstanding citizens, quiet, hard-working types being hauled off by local law enforcement officers in the leafy suburbs north of Chicago, in a trailer park in Fresno, at a hardware store in Moline, at a farmhouse outside of Portland, and in a modest apartment complex in St. Louis. The directive from D.C. that accompanied the warrants was specific. The time of the arrests had to coincide to prevent any sort of warning going out to the others. In reality, the big shots in D.C. need not have worried. None of the Soviet Union's plants had any knowledge of the identity or location of the others. The only time they appeared together was in the log of the late Professor Hartmut Schnelling, a log that continues to yield a treasure trove of information for the country's long-term prosecution of the Cold War.

Yevgeny Kasparanov has survived his first week of arrest and interrogation in the Lubyanka. The KGB has been thorough, if not particularly brutal. That his life has for the moment been spared is a blessing. He knew his arrest was inevitable when news of the shootout on the streets of Atlanta reached his rivals in the Kremlin. He didn't flee, he didn't struggle, and in the end he went without protest. At that point, no one could protect him. Rumors abounded about the tenuous position of the General Secretary in light of the withdrawal from Cuba. The days of his most powerful adherent are probably numbered just as his are. Such is life in the Soviet Union. A once bright political future has been extinguished; the promising career of a true believer has come to an abrupt end. He accepts his fate, and what he craves now more than sunlight, more than an hour of uninterrupted sleep, more than a meal that might make a dent in his hunger, is any bit of news of his family.

Dmitri Bogdonevitch and Yuri Belyavski lean against the freighter's waist-high gunwale, smoking and gazing at the choppy waters of the Atlantic. They're steaming north and east for Gibraltar.

"So much for adventure," Dmitri laments.

"So much for romance," Yuri agrees.

The order to rapidly dismantle the 43rd's weapons for loading and return to Romny was the first welcome bit of news the two men had received since arriving in Cuba.

"Perhaps the next time our glorious leaders decide to send us halfway around the world they'll make sure to send us where we can read the road signs."

"Or where the bugs are smaller than my thumbs."

"Or where more than one or two of the locals will welcome us."

"Dmitri?"

"Yes?"

"Do you know of such a place?"

"I don't. Do you?"

"Of course not. It doesn't exist."

"Then why do we keep looking?"

"Why do you ask such questions?"

"Someone has to."

"That's where you're wrong. If the right questions were asked, you and I would be out of work."

The two men, resigned to accept what life has in store for them, continue to smoke as they and their comrades make their long way home.

Nick and Dalila sit at an Eastern Airlines gate in Washington's National Airport. A DC-7 will take her to Idlewild in New York where she'll catch a flight to Kenya with stops in London and Cairo.

Kyle Richardson and Ted Durant stand to the side. They're here to see Dalila off, but they want to give Nick and Dalila some privacy.

Dalila's hand is in Nick's causing more than a few disapproving glances from passersby. They are both aware of the stares and glares.

"We've still got a long way to go."

"You and me?"

"I meant the country."

"Will you come visit my country?"

"Absolutely, but I wouldn't need to if you'd accept the Director's offer."

"You don't think we could live together here, do you?"

"No. I was thinking about St. Thomas."

"It's a lovely dream, Nick, but I want to return to Kenya."

"Homesick yet?"

"Something like that."

The boarding of Dalila's flight is announced over the public address system. They both stand up. He holds her hands in his.

Nick nods towards the disapproving crowd.

"Want to give them something to talk about?"

"What's in it for me, Mr. Temple?"

"This."

Nick pulls her to him, wraps his arms around her waist and kisses her deeply. They break off the kiss and she leans against his shoulder.

"I shall think of nothing but you the whole way home," she whispers. She backs away and grabs her small flight bag.

"Good bye, Nick. And thank you."

She gives him a peck on the cheek and gets in line to board the aircraft.

Nick, Kyle and Ted watch her as she leaves the building for the tarmac.

"You're a lucky man, Nick Temple."

"You've got that right, Kyle."

The three men turn and head away from the gate for the terminal. Nick masks the emotional depth of the moment by asking casually, "Who needs a drink?"

"You buying?" Ted asks.

"I am. See if you can keep up."

Ted slaps Nick on the back.

"Nick, I'm not even gonna try."

THE END

www.ingramcontent.com/pod-product-compliance
Lightning Source LLC
Chambersburg PA
CBHW071148170626
46809CB00002B/818